PROLOGUE

There was something odd about Geiststadt. Everyone sensed it, although no one could explain exactly what it was. More than anything else, it was a feeling that the place was somehow different: a part of neighboring Brooklyn, and yet strange and peculiar in some indescribable fashion.

People driving through sometimes felt a sudden change in temperature as if they had passed from one climate to another, from heat to cold and back again, instantly and with no warning.

And sometimes a passenger would look out a car window and see something vaguely human in appearance waver in the air like a mirage and disappear, and the short hairs at the base of the passenger's neck would prickle and rise.

—*"Harry! Did you see that?"*

"What, Marie? I'm trying to drive, goddammit."

"In that alley. It was a man, watching us. He was there, and then he was gone. Poof! Just like that."

"Jesus, Marie, you're losing it, you know that? You really are." —

Animals, always attuned to things a little bit beyond human sensibility, were aware of the oddness and avoided Geiststadt when they could. There were few stray dogs to be found there. They preferred to go elsewhere to root through garbage bins or curl up in a spot of shade in the summertime.

Many parts of the surrounding city had a pigeon problem. Not so, Geiststadt. Pigeons found their roosts and built their nests in other places, leaving the few statues in Geiststadt clean and shiny and free of droppings.

Perhaps the stony ridges that helped to somewhat isolate the place had something to do with the feeling of strangeness that pervaded it.

Or perhaps it was the series of interconnected cemeteries that sprouted on its southern border in the middle of the nineteenth century.

It could even have had something to do with Geiststadt's bizarre history, or lack of it. For no one knew the truth of the town's beginnings. It had started out as a small community in the early 1650s, settled by Dutch farmers and named by them Dunkelstad, but that place had simply disappeared, and the people with it. No one knew why. Some historians said there had been a plague. Others said the village had been wiped out by an Indian raid. Still others hinted at darker happenings, though no one said what those might have been.

Whatever the reason for the demise of Dunkelstad, people avoided the area for years after its extinction in spite of the rich, fertile soil, well-watered by Skumring Kill. It was not until the early 1700s that a new wave of

The TWILIGHT ZONE

Book 2
A GATHERING OF SHADOWS

RUSSELL DAVIS

ibooks

new york
www.ibooks.net
DISTRIBUTED BY SIMON & SCHUSTER, INC.

This one's for the gang of three:
Mertz, Crider, and Reasoner
Nobody does it better.

An Original Publication of ibooks, inc.

The Twilight Zone
TM and © 2003 CBS Broadcasting, Inc.
ALL RIGHTS RESERVED.

An ibooks, inc. Book

Distributed by Simon & Schuster, Inc.
1230 Avenue of the Americas, New York, NY 10020

ibooks, inc.
24 West 25th Street
New York, NY 10010

The ibooks World Wide Web Site Address is:
http://www.ibooks.net

ISBN 0-7434-7471-6
First ibooks, inc. printing August 2003
10 9 8 7 6 5 4 3 2 1

Edited by Karen Haber

Special thanks to John Van Citters

Cover design by Joe Bailey
Printed in the U.S.A.

immigrants, this time Palatine Germans, settled in the region and called their new town Geiststadt. Life there was pleasant enough, and events showed no trace of the macabre or outlandish until a hundred years later, when a series of gruesome beheadings distressed the town.

Few people nowadays knew the story of the crimes, which were reminiscent of those attributed to Washington Irving's Headless Horseman. It had been a long time, nearly two hundred years, and the tale had been twisted into urban legend, something that children told each other while huddled beneath their blankets with flashlights to bring gooseflesh to their arms.

– *"I betcha the head-taker is still around here. It was like a ghost or something, and it can't die because it's already dead. I betcha it'll getcha in your bed some night when you're asleep."*

"You're a butthole, Frankie. You don't know about any head-taker."

"Do so. Grampa told me all about it. Said there was just bodies and no heads left. It ate the heads, I betcha."

"Uh-uh."

"OK, have it your way. But I'd sleep with my hands under the covers if I was you. You never know what's hiding under your bed to come out and GETCHA!"

"Mo-o-o-o-om!" –

There were other tales, too, having to do with the two powerful families from Geiststadt's early days, tales of madness and murder that had once been woven into the gossip of the town but were now largely forgotten. After all, who today believes in magic and the power of the supernatural? Descendants of the two once-great families still lived in Geiststadt, but they kept themselves well clear of any idle chatter about what might have happened in the past.

One of the families, the Noirs, was unusual in that there were so many children, thirteen of them, all boys, but most people attributed that fact to a love of family and an adherence to good old-fashioned values of parenthood and filial obedience all too seldom found in these degenerate times. The parents and one son, Mason, still lived in the ancestral home, a dark and foreboding pile of stone and wood that looked quite out of place in the modern town that Geiststadt had become.

The Derlichts as well seemed to believe in the concept of being fruitful and multiplying. The current family was, oddly enough, of the same size as that of the Noirs, with the interesting difference that all thirteen Derlicht children were female. Unlike the Noirs, who took part in the life of the community, the Derlichts had a reputation for keeping to themselves, as if they felt themselves somehow above and apart from their neighbors.

Their home, Derlicht Haus as it was known, was not the original structure dating from the early colonial days. That building had been destroyed in what some said was a terrible fire and others claimed was a storm of preternatural power. But even the new Derlicht Haus was older than most of the other structures in the town, and it seemed continually in shadow, even on the sunniest of days.

Children sometimes referred to it as a haunted house, and for once there was truth in their childish tales. There were ghosts there, as there were in other places in

Geiststadt. And they waited, with the patience of the dead, they waited for *their* time to come.

A time that was now at hand.

CHAPTER ONE

When Antonia Derlicht entered the old building on University Place, male heads turned in her direction. Antonia didn't notice, as she wasn't at all interested in that kind of attention. She didn't even bother to acknowledge it. As a graduate student in New York University's Department of English, she was absorbed in her studies and cared very little about anything else. The young men who had sat in the classroom with her over the years were seriously disappointed by her attitude, but none of them had ever been able to change it.

Her long black hair was thick and lustrous and hung to her shoulders. Today it was a bit windblown, but for some reason that only made her more attractive. Her eyes were as black as her hair, and they sparkled with intelligence. Her lithe figure was hidden beneath the heavy coat she wore against the cold outside, but the men knew that she was put together like a lingerie model.

"What a waste," one of the men muttered, shaking his head as she swept by him and a friend in the hallway.

"Wonder where she's headed in such a hurry?" the other said.

"Probably on her way to see Dr. Martin. That's the only man she's interested in."

"What's he got that we don't have?"

"You mean besides an advanced degree, tenure at a major university, and publications out the wazoo?"

"Yeah, besides that."

"To tell you the truth, I can't think of a single thing."

"Damned shame, then, for sure."

Antonia didn't hear them, of course, but had she heard, she wouldn't have been bothered. She was quite single-minded in the pursuit of her degree, and today she was going to meet with Dr. Martin to discuss her Special Project. It was one of the requirements for the Master's Degree that she was seeking. The Special Project was to be a paper written as part of her Guided Research course, and she had decided on her topic. She had written a shorter paper on the same subject earlier in one of her American literature courses, and she hoped that Dr. Martin, her faculty advisor, would agree that a revision and extension of the paper would be just the thing for her project. She was almost certain that he would, since it had been in his class that she had written the earlier version, which had earned Dr. Martin's praise and a grade of A+ besides.

The door to Martin's office was open, as it always was when he was in the building. He sat at a desk that was covered with a jumble of papers and books. The office was crowded with shelves that held more papers and many more books. On the top of the shelves, the stacked books reached almost to the small room's ceiling.

Martin was a lanky man with a few wisps of hair and a gray, almost white, goatee that he had grown as a very young man, when only beatniks had them. Now that he was old and goatees were fashionable again among athletes and young corporate climbers, Martin had told his class he was considering shaving his. He didn't like the idea of being part of the mainstream. He looked up from the paper he was reading when Antonia tapped on the doorframe of the office.

"Ahh, Miss Derlicht," he said. "Good morning."

Many of Antonia's professors at the university believed in being informal with students and calling them by their first names. Some of them even let the students address them in the same way. But Dr. Martin had never worked that way, and although he openly acknowledged that most of the younger faculty members, and probably most of the students, regarded him as a hopelessly out-of-it geezer, he used formal methods of address. Besides, he'd once said to Antonia during an informal discussion, a man of his age *was* a geezer, and calling students by their given names couldn't possibly change that.

"Good morning, Dr. Martin," Antonia replied.

She had a husky voice that most men would have considered undeniably sexy. Not Dr. Martin, however. One of the things he liked about her was that she cared about her studies, pretty much to the exclusion of everything else, and that she was just as happy to be as formal as he was. He moved some of the student papers out of the chair by his desk into a new stack on one of the shelves nearby.

Antonia she sat down, setting her purse on the floor. She left her coat on because it was chilly in the old building.

"I suppose you're here to talk about your Special Project," Martin said.

Antonia crossed her legs, which might have caused Martin some consternation even at his age had she not been wearing jeans.

"Yes," she said. "I want to rework my paper on urban folklore, the one I did when I was studying Washington Irving with you. Do you remember it?"

"You mean the one about the head-taker?" he said. "While I don't remember every paper I read, yours was most remarkable. It was on the supposed series of murders that mirrored those described in Irving's tale of the Headless Horseman, right?"

"That's right," Antonia said, smiling because he had remembered.

She had a rather severe face, but when she smiled, it relaxed into a very pretty one, and even Martin was conscious of the warmth it brought to her appearance. He shifted uncomfortably in his chair and wished that he hadn't stopped smoking thirty years earlier.

"And how do you propose to expand on your original idea?" he asked.

"I thought it would be interesting to delve into some of the other old stories about my neighborhood," Antonia said. "Geiststadt. I'm sure that there are other stories that tie the Noir family, and even my own, into the folktales and legends that started there in the nineteenth century, and are told today to scare children."

Martin believed in traditional papers, the kind that examined a text and enlightened the reader. He extolled the virtues of this kind of work to his classes, and openly hated what he regarded as faddish schools of critical thought, especially deconstructionist theory and any approach to literature based on politics. But he'd also made clear that he was willing to relax enough to allow someone to do original work as long as the work was at least tangentially related to literature and as long as the student writing it was capable of that level of work—at least, that's what Antonia was betting on.

"I assume that you would be collecting these folktales and including them in your paper," he said.

"Oh, yes. I already have several ideas."

"But you will begin with the Washington Irving story, I hope. We have to be sure that there is a literary component."

Antonia smiled. "That was my plan. I'm very excited about the possibilities of this work. I think it might even be publishable."

"If it is, I'll be glad to suggest some journals that might be interested."

"I was hoping you would. I have a lot of confidence in this project."

"Very well, then," Martin said. "I'll approve it. It's not the usual sort of thing, but I believe you can bring it off. Exactly what kind of research were you planning to do? Interviews? Or are there some historical sources that you're planning to incorporate?"

Antonia's tone became guarded. "I have access to some old documents. Family things."

Martin wasn't sure he liked the sound of that. Research into original documents was fine, if the documents were housed in a reputable library and open to scholarly examination and study. But if they were privately held, there could be a problem.

"I don't want to discourage you," he said, "but you'll have to allow access to those family papers if you plan to publish your work, or even have it approved by the department. Otherwise, my recommendation might not be enough."

"Everything will be documented from impeccable sources," Antonia assured him. "Those old family papers will serve as a starting point to lead me in even more directions."

"Well, then, that's fine," Martin said. "I'm looking forward to working with you on this, Miss Derlicht."

Antonia took hold of the handle of her purse and stood up.

"I'm looking forward to it, too. It's going to be very interesting, I'm sure."

She gave Martin another smile and left the office feeling slightly duplicitous. She had told Dr. Martin the whole truth about her project and her interest in it, but she hadn't told him the truth as a whole.

She strode down the corridor of the old building. While she recognized several faces and nodded to people from some of her classes, she stopped to talk to no one. She had never made friends easily, though she had never understood why. To an outsider, it would have seemed that being part of such a large family might have made her gregarious, but the opposite was true. Where her sisters were good at relating to others, she was often blunt, perhaps in part because of her somewhat sheltered upbringing. As the baby of the family, she had been spoiled and protected by her parents as the others had not.

As a result, she and her sisters had never been close, as all the elder children seemed to regard her as a favorite of their parents and as a rival for their affections. There was a lot more bickering and antagonism than there was nurturing in Antonia's relationships with her older siblings, most of whom fled Geiststadt as soon as they were old enough to leave.

Antonia had never understood their antipathy to the neighborhood, or to her. She loved Derlicht Haus, and when her parents had encouraged her to live there and continue her university studies for as long as she wanted, she jumped at the chance. There was much she wanted to learn about her family's history and its relationship to Geiststadt, and now she was going to delve into something that had recently begun to fascinate her.

It had all started when her father had told her a little of the history behind the stories of the head-taker. Antonia knew that there was, and had been ever since she could remember, a rivalry of some kind between her family and the Noirs, but she had never really understood it. Her father would only say that it "went back a long way." For whatever reason, he seemed to blame the Noirs for the fact that his own family had never achieved the prominence the Noirs had.

"Just look at them," he had said. "They've had state congressmen and even a few judges. A best-selling novelist. CEOs in some of the biggest companies around. The Derlichts have been in this country as long as the Noirs, and our family has must as many talented people, and where have we gotten? Nowhere, that's where we've gotten."

Antonia didn't agree with him, and she wondered if he was bitter because he'd fathered only girl children. After all, one of her sisters was a well-known lawyer in Manhattan, and another of them was an actress who, while she'd never exactly been nominated for an Academy Award, had succeeded in Hollywood and done very well in supporting roles and commercials. Two other sisters were married to prominent businessmen, and all the others were either employed or married or both.

"I think," her father had said, "that if you knew a little more about the history of the two families, you would get a better understanding."

Antonia wasn't sure precisely what he had meant, and perhaps it was the mysterious nature of his comments that had gotten her so interested in the folktales connected to the Noirs and the Derlichts. She even had the vague notion that if she could uncover the true history behind the tales, she might be able to do something to return her own family to prominence and perhaps at the same time make her father proud.

It wouldn't have done to tell any of that to Dr. Martin, however. He wouldn't have understood, and it was none of his business anyway. Besides, he might not have allowed her to do the research if he'd thought it had such a personal basis. Not that she would let personal concerns sway her, she thought. She would do the research, and she would do it right. Scholarship was important to her. And if, in the end, her project provided her with more than merely academic benefits, no one could complain.

The cold wind lifted the corners of her coat when she left the building, and she tugged the garment more tightly around her. The chill in the air felt like something more than winter, and Antonia shivered underneath the wool. For a moment, it felt as if someone had opened her chest and placed an icy finger on her heart.

CHAPTER TWO

Mason Noir sat in the cramped study on the second floor of Noir Manor and looked around him. The room was the largest in Noir Manor, and it had been the place where Captain Benjamin Noir, Mason's great-great-grandfather, had gathered artifacts during his wanderings around the world. Some of those artifacts still remained, though the dust of years covered them and Mason paid them little attention: Tiki heads from Polynesia, busts of long dead Romans and Egyptians whose names were now forgotten by all but the most devoted to the study of those vanished cultures, and in one corner stood an ancient sarcophagus.

It was in this same room that the progenitor of the Noirs had tutored his thirteenth son, Thomas, in the things that Benjamin believed essential for his thirteenth son to know, including Latin, Greek, and other dead languages; mathematics and chemistry; astronomy and astrology; theology and demonology.

Mason could almost feel the presence of his ancestor there with him, could almost hear the old man's voice as he discoursed on the powers and duties that Thomas had fallen heir to by order of birth. For Benjamin, like Thomas after him, and like Mason's father, James, had been a thirteenth son.

And so was Mason. It was the one duty of every thirteenth Noir son to have a like number of male descendants, no matter what. In James's case, it had been difficult because of a condition called *teratospermia*, which meant that more than fifty percent of his sperm had an abnormal shape, making it incredibly difficult for his wives (there had been two) to conceive. But those difficulties had been overcome with the help of many doctors, or so Mason had been told. He suspected that there might have been other kinds of aid invoked as well, for thirteenth sons of thirteenth sons had power. *Heka*, his great-grandfather had called it. It had not been strong in his father, though no one knew why. Perhaps it was related to the teratospermia. At any rate, Mason was expected to be the one who would bring the Noirs the glory they deserved.

For his part, Mason thought the Noirs had glory enough. The family was prominent in the neighborhood, and several of his brothers were nationally known. Popular glory was fleeting, Mason believed, but scientific glory... that could last many, many lifetimes.

That didn't satisfy his father, however. He had often told Mason that the Noirs had an unfulfilled destiny, a destiny that would bring them power known to only a few families in all of history, and he looked to Mason to bring that destiny to fruition. Once, so the family stories ran, Thomas Noir was to have done that, but something had happened, something so terrible that no Noir had spoken of it for over a hundred and fifty years.

Mason didn't know what had happened to Thomas, but from the few dark hints he had picked up, he gathered that Thomas had spent most of his life sequestered within the walls of Noir Manor, never even venturing outside. Perhaps he had spent most of his time in the very study where Mason now sat.

Mason didn't think there was a chance that he would do any better at accomplishing his family's destiny than Thomas had, for the simple fact was that Mason was notoriously bad with women. His luck with women wasn't due to his lack of interest, quite the contrary, but that Mason was something of a nerd. His inherent clumsiness (he tended to be single-minded, and often bumped into things he should have seen but didn't) only enhanced this appearance to those of the opposite gender.

Whereas Benjamin Noir's study, according to family lore, had once been filled with books on the occult and all manner of cabalistic writings, there were no such things in evidence now. For all Mason knew, Thomas had destroyed them, not that it mattered. Mason had no interest in the occult or ancient gods. He put his faith in more modern things, like computers.

On the big wooden desk where Benjamin Noir had once studied moldering texts on ways to transmute gold into lead, Mason had set up his computer system. It was not a commercial product but rather one that Mason had assembled himself, with the fastest chip available, and even that over-clocked, and with the kind of RAM and ROM that the most ardent gamers only dreamed about.

If any of the family's psychic ability was latent in Mason, he hadn't discovered it. Talk of such things reminded Mason of a parlor game, or of the kind of mind-reading act that a second-rate magician would do to entertain a dinner theater crowd. Mason believed that there was more far more *heka* in his computer than in the human mind, and that the glowing screen in front of him was more likely to reveal the secrets of power than any spell or incantation ever devised.

There was a tap at the door, and Mason shook himself out of his reverie. One of his problems was that he was a dreamer. He tended to drift into daydreams when he should have been concentrating on his work.

He turned to the door and said, "Come on in."

The door opened and his father stepped into the room. James Noir was a tall man in his early seventies, thin almost to the point of emaciation. His thin gray hair was combed across his head, and his pink scalp showed through. His eyes were a washed-out blue, and there were dark circles beneath them, but his voice was still strong and commanding.

"So," he said, standing beside his son's chair and looking at the screen filled with symbols that were incomprehensible to him. "I see that you're still not doing any useful work."

Mason had once let such statements bother him, but not any longer. He had heard them too often, and now he simply ignored them.

"You're not a bad-looking boy, you know," James said. "You could be out on a date with some attractive woman."

"I'm not a boy," Mason said. "I'm thirty-two years old."

"All the more reason you should be out on a date," James said.

For several years now, James had been making similar statements. Mason knew why. It wasn't that James had no grandchildren. Mason had so many nieces and nephews that he could hardly keep up with them. But that wasn't enough for James. He wanted his thirteenth son to have children, and a thirteenth son of his own. And if Mason didn't get busy soon, he could have difficulty siring the necessary number.

"Women aren't interested in me," Mason said. "I've tried. It never works out."

"That's because what you call *trying* consists of romancing a woman by talking to her about computer codes," James said. "You have no more idea of romance than a stone."

There was considerable truth in that remark, so Mason didn't even bother to object. He'd never met a woman who really interested him. He knew nothing of the latest television shows, and he hadn't been to a movie in several years. He cared nothing about politics, either local or national, and world events simply didn't concern him. Sports? He could tell the difference between a football and a baseball, but he didn't know which game the New York Jets played. Making small talk on a date was sheer torture for him.

"I have better things to do than to spend my time with someone who doesn't share any of my interests," Mason said.

"Then you'd better find some other interests," James told him. "You'll be thirty-three years old next year, and by that time you must be married."

He didn't say *or else*, but it was implicit in his tone. Mason turned in his chair and, for the first time that afternoon, looked directly at him.

"What are you saying?"

"I'm saying that you're going to have to get out of the chair and away from that screen. That you're going to have to find a wife."

"I told you that women aren't interested in me," Mason said, hating the whiny tone that his voice had taken on but unable to do anything to prevent it.

"They'll be interested in your family and your money, then," James said. "And while we're talking about money, let me tell you right now that I've talked this over with your mother already, so there's no need to go to her. She's in complete agreement with me."

"About what?" Mason asked, feeling as if he'd somehow missed an important part of the conversation.

"About the fact that we'll no longer be funding your researches after this year. You're either to be married, or you'll have to find another source of money."

"But you can't do that."

"I can, and I will. The Noir family will not fail in its destiny because of any son of mine."

Mason's shoulders slumped. "Even if I tried, I couldn't find a wife. You don't know how it is."

"I don't *care* how it is." James turned and left the room. Just outside the door, he turned back and said, "I hope you understand me."

"You've made it clear enough," Mason said.

"Very well. You know what you have to do."

Mason didn't answer. He turned to stare at the computer screen, and his father closed the door.

Mason didn't know how long he sat there, but at some point everything on the screen began to blur, then swirl. The swirling continued for a while—seconds, minutes, hours. Mason had lost all sense of time. Something was happening, something that he didn't understand, and he was powerless to stop it.

As he watched, unable to move, a whirlpool formed on the screen in front of him. It was as three-dimensional as anything Mason had ever seen on a screen, spiraling darkly away from him as if it extended somehow past the back of the flat-panel monitor and away into...somewhere else.

And it was taking Mason with it.

He was aware of a vague sensation of being tugged along an invisible wire, yet was helpless to stop himself from being pulled out of his chair and into the whirlpool.

The scientific, rational part of his brain screamed that what he was experiencing wasn't possible, was patently impossible—a belief he tried to cling to desperately, while he grabbed at the bottom of his chair with equal desperation.

But his fingers might as well have been cooked spaghetti for all the gripping power they had. He rose from the chair and floated toward the monitor, the antique brass key that opened the door to his lab dangled beneath him, swinging like a pendulum from his neck.

His head entered first, somehow fitting itself easily into the black, whirling space.

My shoulders, he thought. *My shoulders will never fit! They'll be broken like old sticks against the monitor!*

But they did, and then his chest, but by that time Mason no longer had any consciousness of his body.

He no longer felt anything at all.

CHAPTER THREE

Antonia parked her gray Camry in the garage that adjoined Derlicht Haus and went into the kitchen, where her father, Frederick, was waiting for her. He was a stout old man, with a full head of thick, wavy hair the color of ash. His face, which had a number of wrinkles, had an anticipatory look.

"Did Dr. Martin approve your Special Project?" Frederick asked.

"Yes," Antonia said. "He questioned me a little about the research materials, but in the end he didn't hesitate about the recommendation."

"Good. I was afraid he might think the subject was too unliterary for the English department."

Antonia smiled at her father and looked around the kitchen. Like everything else at Derlicht Haus, it sparkled with cleanliness. Frederick was fanatical about keeping every room in the house spotless.

"As long as I keep mentioning Washington Irving, I'm in the clear," Antonia said. "But you promised that when the project was approved, you'd tell me why you were so interested in having me pursue this idea. You've been very mysterious about it so far."

Frederick said nothing, and Antonia took her coat into the hallway and hung it in the closet.

"Sit down," Frederick said when she returned to the kitchen. He indicated one of the straight-backed wooden chairs at the old oaken table that had been in the kitchen for all of Antonia's life. It had, in fact, been rescued from the original Derlicht Haus and had remained in the family ever since.

After Antonia was seated, Frederick went to the refrigerator, which, in contrast to the table, was a quite modern side-by-side model, and got out a gallon of milk. Two glasses sat on the marble counter, and he poured milk into both of them. Then he put the milk back in the refrigerator and set the glasses and two napkins on the table.

"What, no cookies?" Antonia said.

She found it amusing that Frederick had tried so hard to be both mother and father after her mother's death two years earlier from cancer. He always liked to talk things over in the kitchen as her mother had done, and always with food of some kind.

"I didn't make cookies," Frederick said, "and you should not make fun of your father."

"I wasn't making fun," Antonia said, taking a sip of the cold milk.

Hot chocolate would have been a more appropriate on such a cold day, she thought, but she didn't say so. She had shaken off the feeling of apprehension that had assailed her after her conversation with Dr. Martin, and she was feeling quite pleased with herself for having succeeded in getting her project approved.

"Good," Frederick said. "You should never make fun of your parents. Respect for family is a wonderful thing. I only wish your mother were here to help us along. She knew far more about the Derlicht family history than even I do, since my mother shared it with her." He sighed, his eyes far away, then added, "Still, she told me enough that I should be able to get you started in the right direction."

Antonia rolled her cold glass slowly between her fingertips, trying to be patient, but failing. "Help us along?" she said. "Why *us*? You're still being too mysterious to suit me."

Frederick had not touched his own glass. Now he picked it up and took a deep swallow of milk. He set the glass down and wiped his mouth with his napkin.

"Since the day of your birth," he said to Antonia, "it has been my—or I should say the family's—wish that someday you would be the one to help restore his family to its rightful place in the world. You are my thirteenth daughter, and it is your duty, and your fate, to do so."

Frederick had never been the jolliest of people, but seldom had Antonia seen him so solemn.

"You make this project sound like it's the most important thing I'll ever do," Antonia said. "It's just a paper about things that have happened around here and how they've been transformed into legends. It's not going to change the world."

"Oh, but that is where you are wrong," Frederick said. "It *is* going to change the world."

Antonia looked at him, wide-eyed, and Frederick smiled fondly at her.

"Maybe not the whole world," he said. "Maybe only our world. But it will change things. You will see."

"But how? I don't understand."

"You see that spot on the table?"

Frederick pointed to a place in the center of the old table that had been repaired with plastic wood at some time in the past, some time long before Antonia had been born.

"I see it," she said. "And I know the story."

According to family legend, some insect had laid an egg in the wood of the tree before it had been cut and made into a table. Years later the heat of a cooking dish on the spot had caused the egg to hatch, and the bug had eaten its way out of the wooden prison to fly away in newfound freedom.

"But I don't see what the story has to do with our family," Antonia said.

"That is because you have not yet done your research."

"You mentioned something about some old family papers that would help me," Antonia said. "But Dr. Martin insisted that everything had to be based on reputable sources."

"Reputable? What is that? I will show you what is reputable. But first, you drink your milk."

Antonia drank her milk, all the time wondering what her father had in mind. Frederick was the one who had encouraged her to do the first paper on the head-taker tale and its similarity to the legend recorded by Washington Irving, and he had not been shy about suggesting that an expansion of that paper would make a wonderful Special Project. And he had further hinted that such a project might have other benefits that had to do with their family. Antonia had been excited at the prospect of the research, and had gone along without protest. Now she was eager to find out exactly what was behind her father's hints and insinuations.

She set the milk glass down on the table with a solid *thunk* and wiped her mouth to be sure she didn't have a milk moustache. "I'm finished," she said. "Now stop being so cryptic and tell me what you have in mind."

"You have never taken much interest in your family's heritage," Frederick said. "I hoped this project would be the thing to kindle your desire to learn more about your ancestors, about their lives and what they did here in Geiststadt when the town was new."

Antonia nodded. She had never cared much for ancient history unless it related to some story or poem she was reading. What her family had been or done didn't enter into her thinking.

"Today you will begin learning more," Frederick said. "You will find out how great the Derlichts were, long ago, and how the Noirs"—his mouth twisted as he said the name—"how the Noirs nearly destroyed us."

"Why haven't you told me any of this before?"

"Because the time was not yet right. As I have said, you were not interested in your heritage. You always had your nose in a book, as if the world between the covers was more real than this one. Today you will learn that this world, or at least a certain part of it, is as fascinating as anything you have ever read about."

Antonia's interest was piqued, and she hoped that Frederick would continue.

But he was not quite ready to explain to her just what he had in mind. He pushed his chair back from the table and took the glasses to the sink, where he rinsed them carefully before putting them into the dishwasher.

When that was done, he straightened up and said, "Come. We will go to the attic."

Despite the small chill that ran on mouse feet up her spine, Antonia was further intrigued. The attic had been off limits to her for all her life. She had been up the stairway leading up to it several times, on dares from her older sisters, but she had never opened the door at the top. That had never been allowed, and she had never really even considered it, especially after one of her sisters, Amanda, had one day gone up the stairs and turned the doorknob. She had pushed the door partway open, but she had been so frightened by whatever she had seen there that she had not gone inside, and in fact she had never spoken about the incident except to warn Antonia that she should never disobey her parents and try to enter that room. Amanda, though not the oldest of the sisters, had been the first to leave Derlicht Haus when she came of age. And she had never returned.

"I've never been to the attic," Antonia said.

"I know," Frederick told her. "It has been forbidden to you."

"But we're going there now?"

"Yes. I should have said, it is forbidden to all who do not go there for a certain purpose. Which is why we are going. Otherwise it is dangerous."

"Dangerous?" Antonia thought again of Amanda and the terrified look upon her face when she had spoken of opening that door. "How is it dangerous?"

"You will see," Frederick said. "Come along."

He walked out of the kitchen, his back straight.

As Antonia watched him go, she felt once again the iciness at the very core of her being.

She shivered. And then followed her father down the hallway and to the stairs that led to the attic.

CHAPTER FOUR

Awareness returned to Mason with a rush of feeling so intense that he felt almost as if he had been blown to bits and somehow reassembled in the very instant of his destruction.

He was whirling down a corridor of darkness, but there were niches in the corridor's walls. In the niches were busts that he thought he would recognize if he were going more slowly, and with that thought his progress slowed considerably. He tried to focus on the busts, and when he did, he saw that they were the Tiki heads from the study, and others as well. There were some that he did not recognize, and all of them regarded him with eyes that glowed from within their sockets with a light that was hideously red and alive.

The corridor changed. It was no longer dark. It glowed like the eyes in the heads, but they were no longer in evidence. There was nothing around Mason but the light. He was drowning in it.

And then he was drowning in water. The warm fluid surrounded him, pressed against him insistently, filled his nose and his eyes, and he opened his mouth to scream.

The water gushed into his mouth and choked him and he died.

And lived again. He was lying on what might have been a beach, for it was sand that stretched before him as far as he could see, lone and level sand, and in the middle of it stood a figure of something almost human. But not quite. It was a figure of Anubis, the jackal-god of Egyptian mythology. As Mason watched another figure appeared beside it, a figure that looked somehow familiar, and then Mason realized it was himself.

Or not himself, for the man was dressed in the fashion of an earlier century. Around him, there was an emanation of power, dark and fluid, like a second set of invisible clothing.

Anubis grinned at Mason with a dogish grin, and his red tongue lolled out of the side of his mouth. Then he spoke, but Mason did not recognize the words.

"He asks if you know him," the man beside Anubis said, and Mason understood the words that he spoke, though they did not sound like American English. They were more like English as it would have been spoken in America's colonial years.

Mason struggled to his feet. "I know him. I've seen pictures of him in books. But he's not real, and I don't know how he got in my dream."

The man laughed. "This is no dream, Mason Noir. Do you know who I am?"

That the man knew his name was for some reason no surprise. Mason said, "You look like me." He was a large man, with dark hair and eyes like pools of jet. His craggy features lent him a rather sinister appearance, and his size enhanced this. *Funny*, Mason thought, *on me it just looks clumsy, while on him, it looks exactly right.*

"On the contrary," said the man, smiling, "you look much like me, for I am older by far than you. I am Thomas Noir."

"Thomas Noir? Then you're dead."

"Not exactly," Thomas said, and he laughed again. The laugh was rueful this time. "Though I have often wished I was. You are the one who can change that wish to something more hopeful."

I'm dreaming, Mason told himself. *I'm sitting in the study asleep, and all my father's nagging has caused me to have some kind of a horrible dream, and when I wake up, it will all be—*

"You are not dreaming," Thomas said, interrupting his thought. Anubis barked a laugh.

"Then how can you read my mind?"

"There are more things in heaven and earth, young Mason, that you have dreamt of in your philosophy."

"Now you're stealing from Shakespeare."

"At least you are well read in a field other than those relating to your machines," Thomas said.

And he was correct, for while Mason cared little for any other arts, he was interested in literature, having learned to read at an early age. He had liked the logical way words flowed together to create meaning.

"Do you know where you are?" Thomas asked.

Mason looked around, then back at Thomas.

"You already know what I think. Why should I repeat it aloud?"

"But you are not in a dream," Thomas said. "Try again."

"I can't think of anything else it could be. What seemed to happen to me is impossible. No one can get sucked into a computer monitor. And don't start quoting Shakespeare to me again."

Thomas looked a bit chagrined, and Anubis laughed again.

"Very well," Thomas said. "I will tell you where you are. Anubis, as you may know, is the guide to the dead in the Underworld."

"So you're telling me that I'm dead?"

"No," Thomas said, "At least... not yet. You are in the Hall of the Judgment, where your eternal fate will be decided. On the one hand, you may find yourself exterminated. On the other ..."

"I can't believe this," Mason said. "You aren't really here, and neither am I."

Again Anubis laughed, as if he understood. Perhaps he, too, was reading Mason's mind.

And again Thomas contradicted Mason.

"I am here in front of you, and as real as your own hand." Thomas held up his own large fist as if to illustrate his point, then suddenly it shot forward slamming into Mason's breastbone with enough force to knock the wind out of him. He doubled over, gasping for breath.

"In this world, I am as real as you, but much more dangerous than you've ever dreamed possible. This is the moment of your decision, Mason Noir, and what you decide, should you decide poorly, may cost you your very life."

Mason managed to suck in enough air to reply, but just as he started to say something, he saw a wavering in the air in back of Thomas and Anubis. It was a flickering of color as if heat waves were rising from the ground, or as if a mirage were about to form.

Anubis and Thomas noticed the direction of Mason's gaze and turned to see what he was looking at.

When they did, a harsh cry came from Anubis and echoed over the barren sands.

The mirage, or whatever it was, began to take a more definite shape, the shape of a man. He looked a bit like Thomas, though his hair was much lighter, his features less edged in appearance.

"You must leave," the man said, staring straight into Mason's eyes. "Leave now."

Mason would have been glad to leave, or wake up, or do whatever he needed to do in order to be back in his chair in the second-floor study at Noir Manor, but he had no clue as to how he could possibly get there.

As soon as the words were out of the other man's mouth, Thomas leapt at him. "You'll not thwart me this time!" he screamed, fastening his fingers on the man's throat. As the other man was borne to the sand, he made a gesture with his right hand, and something exploded in Mason's head. Everything went black.

Again, consciousness returned with a rush, and Mason found himself drowning in the water again, but before he did, he was drowning in the light. And when the light was gone, he was whirling down the dark corridor. This time the faces in each niche seemed to be laughing at him as he tumbled by them in the darkness.

After an interminable time had passed, Mason saw a light in the distance, and he knew that he was being drawn to it. As he got closer and closer to the source of the light, he could see that it was a small rectangular window, and he straightened his limbs so that he could pass through it.

But then he saw that it was much too small. His body would never fit, and he tried to slow himself. He found that he could not, so he put his arms tight to his sides and braced himself for the inevitable collision.

The expected impact never occurred, however. When he reached the window, his head burst through it soundlessly, and Mason saw the study wall. He opened his mouth to cry out, but no sound came from him as he shot from the computer monitor as if from the mouth of a cannon.

He ducked his head as he passed over his chair, and when he landed on the floor, he somersaulted into the wall with a thud. Then he collapsed in a heap on the floor.

How long he lay there, he never knew. He tried several times to get up, but found that he ached all over, ached in places that he'd never ached before. He felt like someone had pounded him with a rubber hammer.

So he sprawled on the floor and tried to figure out what had happened to him.

Had he really seen Thomas Noir? And Anubis? And if he had, who had the third figure been?

Of course he hadn't seen them, he told himself. There was no Anubis, no Thomas Noir, no third person who had materialized out of the desert air. But Mason had certainly experienced something. Could it be that he did have psychic powers? Could he communicate with the dead?

It was too much. Mason had never had a migraine in his life, but now he thought his forehead might crack in two. He groaned and closed his eyes.

They popped open again at once. He was afraid to go to sleep, afraid that he might return to the strange dream-like place from which he had just escaped. He did not want that to happen.

Someone rattled the door of the study. Mason tried again to get up from the floor, but he was powerless to move. The bones might as well have been removed from his legs for all the good they did him.

"Mason! Are you in there?"

It was his father's voice. Mason tried to say that he was there, but his voice, like his legs, failed him.

He lay back on the floor, closed his eyes, and let the darkness take him once again.

CHAPTER FIVE

The stairs that led up to the attic of Derlicht Haus were not as steep as they had once seemed to Antonia, and the light on the stairway was much better. She always thought of the stairs as being in shadow, but sunlight came in through a high window, and she could see that the stairs, like the rest of the house, were spotless.

The door at the top was set into the wall. It was brown and heavy and looked quite solid. There were enigmatic figures carved on it, figures that Antonia didn't recognize. She wasn't sure they were intended to represent anything in particular, but she remembered that they had seemed quite frightening when she was young.

Frederick led the way, and when he reached the final step, he reached into his pocket and removed a heavy brass key of an intricate design. He inserted it into the lock and gave it a turn.

It turned smoothly and without sound, and Frederick removed it from the lock and put it back into his pocket. He palmed the knob of the door, and Antonia felt her heartbeat speed up. Suddenly she wasn't at all sure that she wanted to see what was inside the attic room.

Frederick didn't share her apprehension. He turned the knob and pushed the door open.

The room behind it was dark, and a dank, musty smell came from it. Antonia could hardly believe there was a part of the house that smelled musty. She would have thought that Frederick was too fastidious to allow it.

However, the smell didn't seem to bother him. He entered the room and switched on a light.

"What are you waiting for?" he said, and Antonia mounted the last couple of steps.

Her legs failed her at the threshold. Her muscles refused to obey her brain's command to move her forward.

"It's all right," Frederick said. "It's safe now."

There was an emphasis on the word *now* that Antonia didn't like, but she managed to force her reluctant body through the door and into the room.

There was room for her to stand erect beside her father, though her head almost touched the ceiling, which was nothing but bare boards. They hadn't thought of insulation when Derlicht Haus had been built, and though the lower floors had been improved over the years, no one had done anything to the attic, except to add the light that Frederick had switched on. Even at that, it was just a bare bulb screwed into a socket that hung from a braided electrical cord that must have been at least seventy or eighty years old. The cord was frayed in places, though not quite enough for the bare wires to show through. Antonia wondered if it was safe.

The room itself was as musty as it smelled. Dust motes danced in the light, and Antonia sneezed.

"I don't clean this room," Frederick said.

Antonia believed him. There were windows, but the dust and grime were so thick upon them that she was sure they had not been touched since the house was built. They allowed hardly any outside light into the room. Dirt lay thick on the windowsills and had settled to the cracks of the wooden flooring. Dust puffed up under Antonia's feet with each step.

"I don't come here," Frederick said, stating the obvious. "Not unless it is necessary."

Antonia concentrated on stifling another sneeze. When she had it under control, she said, "And it's necessary now?"

"Yes. As you can see."

Frederick made a sweeping gesture with his hand, and Antonia looked in the direction he indicated. The room was bare, for the most part, with nothing to see but exposed lumber, but on one wall were bookshelves. And on the shelves were dust-covered, leather-bound volumes that appeared not to have been opened in a hundred years or more. Spider webs hung from the ceiling and some of the books. Antonia brushed at one that threatened to catch in her hair. It came loose from the ceiling and stuck to her fingers.

"I'm not sure I see why it's necessary to be here at all," Antonia said, brushing at the spider web to get it off.

"The books," Frederick said. "Or rather the ledgers, for they are not published manuscripts. They contain the record of our family from the early days, after Derlicht

Haus was rebuilt. And the record of other things as well. They will prove to be quite valuable for your Special Project."

It seemed to Antonia that the words *Special Project* had taken on a meaning quite different from those she and Dr. Martin had been using earlier that day. And she wasn't sure she liked it.

"So we weren't allowed in here as children because we might have disturbed the books?" she said.

Frederick nodded. "That is true. At least it is partially true."

Antonia didn't really think she wanted to know what the other part was, but she asked anyway.

"The room is haunted," Frederick said in a matter-of-fact tone.

Hoping that she hadn't heard him correctly, Antonia said, "Pardon me?"

"Haunted," Frederick repeated.

"Haunted?" she said.

Frederick turned to look directly at her.

"Yes," he said firmly. His eyes seemed to shine with reflected light. "Haunted. Not by the kind of ghosts that you read about in your books, but real ghosts." He paused and turned to look at the quaint and curious volumes on the shelves. "As I told you, the real world can hold far more of interest than anything you have read in your studies thus far."

Antonia waved her hand in front of her face to clear away the dust that she smelled so strongly.

"I don't believe in ghosts," she said.

"Let me tell you a story," Frederick said. "There was a

terrible fire, which you will read about, that destroyed the first Derlicht Haus. But somehow, incredibly, the attic remained almost completely intact. I know that seems impossible to you, but it is true. And the wood from that attic was used in the construction of this one, recreating it almost exactly as it had been."

"What was so special about the attic that allowed it to survive a fire?" Antonia asked.

"No one really knows the answer to that question. Perhaps it was the fact that Agatha Derlicht was confined there. And that she was saved from the fire by—but never mind that. You will find out for yourself soon enough. And perhaps you will find out even more."

"But what about the haunting part?"

"It is said that Agatha Derlicht is still with us. She has not been seen recently, though there are sometimes other signs of her presence. Perhaps you have felt them."

Antonia remembered times when strange things had happened in the old house. Walking from one room to another, she had passed through something that felt like a thin, cold mist, when there was nothing at all to be seen. And at other times she had noticed that things might be moved around in a room, yet no one could re-call having moved them. Antonia had always considered herself a little too grounded to believe that such things were caused by a ghost. Now, she wasn't so sure.

"If the ghost was roaming around the house," she said, "why couldn't we come in this room?"

"Because in this room Agatha retains most of her power. It might not be safe here for someone whose presence was not approved."

"And mine is?"

"Now it is. Now that you are going to be doing the work that needs to be done for our family."

Antonia was not sure how she was supposed to do any research in that room. The light was bad, and it was far too dusty. At that thought, she sneezed again.

"I can't work in here," she said. "We'll have to move the books downstairs."

"Oh, no, we must never do that," Frederick told her. "The books must remain here. You must study them here. You may take notes, but you cannot remove the books."

Antonia didn't like the sound of that.

"Why not?" she asked.

"Because you will be getting special assistance here."

It was hard for Antonia to picture her father helping her with her research, and it was even harder to picture him spending any length of time in a room that was so filthy that it would take days of cleaning just to settle the dust.

"You're going to help me?" she said.

"No. Not I. But someone will."

She was going to ask who he meant, but then it came to her. He was talking about the ghost of Agatha Derlicht. Antonia laughed. She'd already told her father that she didn't believe in the manifestation of spirits, though he didn't appear to have listened. Whatever else happens, Antonia thought, I won't be getting any help from a ghost.

And then she thought once more about Amanda and of her behavior after looking into the attic room. Had she seen the ghost of Agatha Derlicht? Antonia didn't want to believe it, but Amanda had been frightened enough to warn Antonia and her other sisters about the room, and she had avoided the attic forever after.

"I'd really rather take the books downstairs," Antonia said. "I'd be more comfortable there, and I'm not sure I want any assistance."

But Frederick remained firm. He told her again in no uncertain terms that the books could not, would not, be removed from the attic room.

Antonia saw then that arguing would do her no good. She hated the thought of being cooped up in the moldy, dusty attic, but there was no help for it. Now that she knew what her father had meant about helping out the family by researching her project, she had to get to those books and find what secrets they held about the Derlichts. And about the Noirs.

"All right," she said. "You win. I'll do the research here, but we'll have to bring some chairs and a table. The battery in my laptop is good for several hours, but it wouldn't hurt to have another electrical outlet, either. And a portable CD player so I can have some music while I work."

She had a couple of other ideas as well, but she stopped speaking when she noticed that Frederick was shaking his head.

"What?" she said.

"You cannot bring those things up here. The computer, the CD player, they're not allowed. A table, yes, and a chair. A pad of paper to write on, and a pencil. A pen, even. But not the other things."

Antonia was puzzled and worried. She wasn't sure

she'd be able to function without her laptop, and she had always found listening to music a help when spending long hours pouring over research materials

"What's the problem?" she asked. "If you're worried about the electrical wiring, don't. We don't have to put in another outlet. I'll just recharge the computer every day, and it will be all right. I don't have to use it for too many hours each time. And the CD player will run for quite a while on a few batteries."

"When I say you cannot use them, I mean it literally. They will not work here. I am surprised that the light works, but perhaps even a ghost likes light now and then. Or it might be possible that light is permitted because it is absolutely necessary to your task. The windows"—Frederick waved a hand in their direction—"would never permit enough light in here for reading."

"You're saying I can't use a computer and a CD player because a ghost might not like them? That's ridiculous. And we could clean the windows if we had to."

Frederick smiled and looked at his daughter with genuine affection.

"We do not want to change things any more than absolutely necessary. And we do not want to upset Agatha. She can be...quite unpleasant when that happens."

"You talk as if you know her."

"In a manner of speaking, I do know her. As you will before you are done."

Antonia wasn't at all sure she wanted to know Agatha. But she had to admit the prospect was tantalizing. Besides, there was so much history in those old books. Who could say what secrets they might hold about the urban legends of Geiststadt and how those legends began.

"I guess I'll have to do it your way," Antonia said with a grin.

"Not my way," Frederick said. "Agatha's way."

"Agatha's way, then. But no matter whose way it is, we have to bring a table and a chair up here, if nothing else."

"That will be simple enough," Frederick told her. "And not objectionable. As a matter of fact, I have them already waiting for you. They are in the downstairs closet. We will go and get them now."

"You were sure I'd do it, weren't you?"

"And why not? You have always had the curiosity of a scholar, and what scholar could resist an opportunity like this one?"

"Not me," Antonia said. "Not on your life."

"I would not put it quite that strongly if I were you," Frederick said, looking around as if expecting to see someone else there with them. "It is not...proper."

I can see I have a lot to learn about the etiquette of ghostly encounters, Antonia thought as they descended the stairs. And she wasn't at all sure that she wanted to learn it. Not in the way it appeared that she would.

CHAPTER SIX

Mason was aware that someone, or something, was pushing him away from the wall, but he had no idea who, or what it was. His eyes were closed, and he lay in the floor limp as an eel and let himself be moved without trying to resist.

"Mason," his father said from somewhere above him. "Mason, what happened?"

Mason tried to answer, but nothing came out of his mouth but a strangled croak. He felt his father's hands slip under his arms, and then he was being lifted up. He found that he could stand with help, but it required a considerable effort on his part, as his legs threatened to collapse beneath him like boiled linguine. James supported him and helped him over to the computer chair. Mason slid into the chair and held onto the desk to keep himself somewhat erect.

He looked into the monitor and moaned, shoving himself away from the desk with more power than anyone would have expected. The chair rolled backward and struck the wall. Mason bounced forward and fell out of the chair onto the floor.

"Mason," James said, picking him up again and propping him against the wall. "What happened in here? What's the matter with you?"

Again Mason tried to answer, but his voice wheezed out in an incomprehensible breath. His throat felt as if he had swallowed some of the sand he had seen in his vision.

Or was it a vision? It seemed far too real to Mason to have been anything less than an actual event. And could he have envisioned himself being ejected from the computer monitor and tossed halfway across the room? No, but it couldn't have happened, either. Nevertheless, it had. Or something had. Mason's head spun with the implications.

James left the room and came back in a few seconds with a glass of water. He handed it to Mason, but Mason's hands were shaking so badly that the water slopped over the rim of the glass. James took the glass back from Mason and held it to Mason's lips.

"Drink this," he said, and tilted the glass.

The glass clinked against Mason's teeth, but he managed to get some of the water down his throat. He could feel its cool liquidity as it flowed into him. His hands became steadier, so he took the glass from James and drank all the water that was left in it.

When he was finished, he handed the glass to James, who set it on the desk.

"Are you feeling any better now?" James asked.

"Not much," Mason said. His voice sounded a little like the cawing of a feeble crow. "I...something happened."

"Obviously," James said. "Can you tell me what it was?"

"I was swallowed by the monitor," Mason said, and bit by bit he told the story with his strained voice. He paused often to take a deep breath before continuing.

James went out for water twice, and each time Mason drank the whole glassful.

"I know it couldn't have happened," Mason said, shaking his head. "I must have imagined it all. But it seemed very real at the time."

"Oh, it happened, all right," James told him. "No hallucination would have affected you so strongly, no matter what drugs might have induced it."

Mason pushed himself away from the wall and made an effort to stand. His knees felt like sponges, but he was able to stand on his own and walk to his chair. He drooped into it and put his head in his hands.

"I don't use drugs," he mumbled, wondering if perhaps someone had slipped something into his food. That was ridiculous, of course, and he disregarded the thought.

James said, "You know that Thomas, your ancestor who spent much of his life in this very room, was responsible for what happened, don't you?"

Mason shook his head. "It was only a dream," he said, more to himself than in response to what his father had said.

"In Geiststadt, the dead are never very far from the living," James said. "They're all around us, even the ghosts of the old Dutch settlers up on HangedMan's Hill. That's where the White Lady is sometimes seen."

Mason had visited that particular cemetery occasion-

ally when he was a teenager and more likely to leave
the house than he was now. The cemetery overlooked
Skumring Kill and was not too far from Derlicht Haus.
Of course Mason had not gone there to commune with
ghosts, but rather with a different kind of spirits, those
of a more substantial and alcoholic nature. The young
people of Geiststadt found HangedMan's Hill a fine and
private place for certain recreations, and they had never
minded that its real purpose was something a bit more
macabre than anything they intended to do there. No
one of Mason's acquaintance had ever seen the White
Lady.

"Ghosts *don't* exist," Mason said. "They're... they're
figments of an overactive imagination, or plasma gases
caught in light, or one of a hundred other things. *They're
not real.*"

"Who are you trying to convince?" James asked, then
shook his head. "Never mind. What else did Thomas say
to you?"

"Thomas told me I had to make a decision," Mason
said.

"What decision?" James asked.

"He didn't say," Mason said. "The other fellow showed
up before he could clarify what he meant."

"Probably his brother, Jonathan. They were blood enemies, according to family legend."

"It was a dream," Mason reiterated. "Just a dream."

"Okay," James said. "Let's suppose for a minute that
it was just a dream. Will you at least acknowledge that
maybe the dream was trying to tell you something?"

"That's a bit Freudian for my taste," Mason said, "but

49

I'll go along. The dream was trying to tell me something, but what?"

"Maybe," James said, "his interest is in your work. You said he made reference to your knowledge of machines. He must know, somehow, about MIND-NET."

"I thought we'd agreed that the dream was trying to tell me something, *not* Thomas Noir—who is, by the way, dead."

James nodded. "Fair enough. But what else do you really do, Mason, other than work on MIND-NET and read? What other machines are you involved in?"

Mason slumped over in the chair. How could it be possible? Only three people in the world, Mason and his parents, knew about MIND-NET.

"How could he know?" he asked, then corrected himself. "What about MIND-NET would I be trying to tell myself?"

"Forget the convolutions, Mason," James snapped. "For a moment, just try to stretch your mind around the possibility that maybe, just maybe, Thomas Noir, or at least his spirit form, is interested in you, okay?"

Mason shook his head. "All right, fine," he said. "Let's play a fun-filled game of paranormal investigator, where the winner is the one with the least amount of protoplasm on his shirt on the end of the day!"

James grinned. "Let me ask you something, Mason."

"What?" Mason said.

"If what you had was a dream, what's that?" he asked, pointing to Mason's shoes.

"What's what?" Mason asked, bending over to look. Then he saw it.

In the laces of his shoes, fine pieces of sand were plainly visible, the quartz winking back in the dim light of the study like tiny, malevolent eyes.

"I ..." Mason said, trying to speak around the thickening in his throat. "I don't know."

James looked at Mason's shoes a moment more, then said, "I do."

A short time later, Mason was still trying to deny what he'd experienced—at least to himself—while his father continued to talk. *That sand could've come from...from anywhere*, Mason tried to reason with himself. *I could have picked it up outside in the gardens.*

"According to the old family stories," James was saying, "Thomas was a remarkably manipulative character. He would make it a point to know about something like MIND-NET. Especially if he thought he could turn it to his advantage in some way."

Turning his attention back to his father's lecture, Mason thought about his pet project. MIND-NET was still in its early, and highly theoretical, stage of development. At this point, it was more than an idea on paper, but not by much. Still, Mason believed it could be the key to something truly amazing: eternal life.

In its simplest form, the theory of MIND-NET was that since the brain emitted electrical impulses, it should be possible not only to monitor them but perhaps to interpret, record, and then convert them to digital signals. The same binary signals used by computer systems. If it worked as Mason planned, MIND-NET would allow someone to download his own brain waves—his psyche, his memories, even his personality—into a computer system, thus preserving it as long as the system had power. And there were other methods of working with the electrical output of the brain as well. Mason was working on those, too. Furthermore, if MIND-NET could be combined with some of the cloning techniques he knew other scientists were working on, then those recorded bits of data that made up a person could be loaded into a brand new body.

The possibilities were staggering to consider.

"What possible good," Mason asked, "could MIND-NET be to a ghost? No brain, no electrical impulses, nothing that can be recorded."

"Perhaps he believes that you could still tap into his mental energy," James said. "Judging from what just happened here, Thomas's psychic energy pervades this house. And without much doubt his spirit is still around. Corporeal or not, Thomas must still have enough...life, such as his must be, to want more. If you could somehow put him into a new body, he might yet realize his goal of living once more."

"We don't even know that is his goal," Mason said. "And besides, he isn't real!"

James nodded. The family stories about Thomas Noir merely said that he had sought power and that somehow he had become a prisoner in his own house. Exactly how that had happened wasn't part of the tale, though it was said to have been unfortunate for him, and the family as well.

"Who was the other man in whatever it was that I

saw?" Mason asked, still not willing to say that it had been anything more than a dream or vision.

"Probably Jonathan, Thomas' twin brother. There was some kind of rivalry between them. Jonathan died young, but no one knows just how or why."

"He didn't want Thomas to talk to me."

"I wish I could explain it all to you," James said. "But I don't know much more about it than you. My own father never wanted much to discuss things of that nature with me, perhaps because of my...weakness."

There was an awkward pause. James and Mason had never really talked about James' lack of *heka*, though of course his own failings made it all the more important to him that Mason fulfill the family destiny, whatever that might be.

For his part, Mason had been quite shaken by his experience in the computer monitor. Whether it had been real or imagined didn't really matter, he supposed. The important thing was to determine how it had effected him and in what ways. The only way he knew to do that was with MIND-NET.

As someone who had never put much credence in his family's supposed psychic powers, Mason found it quite a shock to come face to face with a dead ancestor, or maybe even two of them, and to believe that it might very well be more than some kind of strange dream.

"I'm having a lot of trouble getting adjusted to this," Mason said. "I'm not convinced it wasn't a dream of some kind. A very strange, very powerful dream."

"I don't blame you," James said. "I can remember some of my own early experiences, even if they weren't quite as intense as yours. It may be that you do have *heka*, Mason, and that it's as strong in you as it was in Thomas or even Benjamin Noir."

Mason didn't want to think about that possibility. He wasn't interested in psychic power, and didn't believe in it. He had his own experiments to think about, and while they might have seemed just as far-fetched to some people as a psychic journey in a computer monitor seemed to him, they were something he could understand and deal with. Or at least he could deal with them if there wasn't any interference from the spirit world that now appeared to be a threatening reality to him.

Then something else occurred to him.

"If Thomas thinks that MIND-NET is important," he said, "maybe I'm on the right track. Otherwise he wouldn't expend the energy he did to reach me."

"I'm afraid you're right," James said.

Mason didn't like to hear his father use the word *afraid*, not even casually.

"What do you mean?" he asked.

"I mean that something is stirring in Geiststadt, something strong and menacing. What just happened to you, and there's no doubt in my mind that it *did* happen, is a sure sign that formidable powers are gathering. It could be that they were roused by MIND-NET, or it could be that there are other things going on, things that we don't yet know about."

"What kind of things?"

"Who can say? What we do know is that whether you want to or not, you're going to be a part of the action.

Thomas might have lost contact with you this time, but he'll be back. You can count on that much."

Mason shuddered. "I don't want him—whatever he is, a dream or some kind of ghost—to come back."

"What you want has nothing to do with it. He'll come at a time of his own choosing, and you'll have no more warning than you did just now, not unless you do something about it."

"What can I do? I've heard stories about ghosts in Geiststadt, but I never really believed in them. I don't know anything about avoiding ghostly manifestations or dealing with them if they show up."

"Yet somehow you managed to escape from the monitor," James said.

"I didn't have anything to do with that. I was sent back."

"Then maybe you'll have help again," James said. He looked around the room as if someone else might be lurking there, someone who could see them talking and hear every word. "You'll have to pray that you do."

Mason wasn't encouraged. He didn't put much stock in praying, no more than he put in ghosts. He believed in things he could see and touch and hear rather than in some vague being that you might address in a religious manner.

But, he thought, half an hour earlier he hadn't believed in some sort of psychic realm that could be reached through a computer monitor, the way that Alice had gone through the looking-glass. It was beginning to become apparent to Mason that the fact of his belief or disbelief didn't mean a thing in the face of the supernatural reality he was now encountering.

And if James was right, it was a reality that had something to do with his own world and his own interests. It was also a reality that could prove highly dangerous, filled with people, or spirits if that's what they were, like that of Thomas Noir, who wanted to force Mason to make some as yet unspecified decision of great importance.

The presence of Anubis hinted to Mason that the decision was a life and death matter, and suddenly Mason remembered what Thomas had said about being Mason's choice costing his own life. Thomas had been about to say more, but he had been interrupted at that point, by Jonathan or whoever it might have been. Could Thomas have meant that if Mason made the wrong choice, Mason himself would be blotted out of existence? And that if he made the right one, he would live forever? It made sense, if you related it to MIND-NET, but Mason wasn't quite ready to accept that Thomas even existed, let alone knew about MIND-NET.

Thinking about it made Mason's head hurt. Or maybe his head hurt because he'd been flung from a computer monitor and then slammed himself up against the wall. Either way, he wasn't feeling his best.

"I think I need another drink," Mason said.

James took the glass from the desk.

"I'll get it for you," he said.

Mason stood up on shaky legs.

"This time I'm going to need something a bit stronger than water."

"I think we can both use it," James said, and the two left the study.

When they went out the door, Mason flipped the light switch and the room darkened, though not entirely. On the desk, the monitor flickered with a blue, uncertain light.

CHAPTER SEVEN

A ntonia placed the metal folding chair at the card
table her father had brought to the attic. Already
on the table was one of the heavy volumes from
the bookshelves. It was bound in leather, and Antonia
had not yet opened it, though her father had cleaned
some of the dust, dirt, and spider webs from it with a
soft cloth. He had treated the book as if it was some rare
treasure, and Antonia supposed that in a way it was.

Also on the table were a lined yellow pad and a pencil.
There was nothing rare or treasured about them. The pad
was the standard eight-and-a-half by eleven inches rather
than the oversized kind known as a legal pad. Antonia
wondered idly if that meant it was an illegal pad. She
didn't suppose it made any difference. A pad was a pad.
She felt a little bit lost without her thin laptop, and she
hoped that she would soon get used to taking notes with
the pencil, though it seemed like a slow, old-fashioned
way to work.

The light that dangled from the ceiling on its frazzled
cord seemed to move slightly now and then as if there
were a breeze blowing through the cracks in the attic

wall. It made shadows all over the attic, and Antonia didn't like that any more than she liked the pad and the pencil. She was used to working in modern libraries with their cold, even, virtually shadow-free illumination. Sterile? Maybe, but that was an atmosphere a lot more conducive to productive work than one in which nearly every breath made your eyes water and in which inhaling the dust gave you a strong urge to sneeze.

And what about the spiders? Antonia wondered. Spiders didn't do a lot to contribute to scholarship in her opinion. What with all the spider webs, there should be a few spiders about, but she hadn't seen any.

Naturally, as soon as the thought occurred to her, she noticed a movement along a baseboard. She turned and saw a fat black spider scuttling along the old floorboards. It disappeared into one of the numerous cracks in the wall, which was some comfort to Antonia, if a small one. At least that particular spider wouldn't be swinging from a web and landing in Antonia's hair or, worse, her face. The thought of the sticky webbing on her skin gave her a creepy feeling, but she disregarded it. She told herself that she was a rational, sensible person and that she had nothing to fear either from spider webs or spiders.

After another glance around the room, she thought that there was no use in putting her research off any longer. She sat down in the chair and pulled the old book to her. She put a finger under the thick cover and hefted it. The leather was well preserved. There were no cracks at all that Antonia could see, which was surprising when you considered the lack of insulation in the attic.

Antonia was going to flip the cover open, but just as

she decided to do so, the weight disappeared from her finger, and the cover opened of its own accord. Antonia jumped in surprise, letting out a little squawk of alarm. Then she took a deep breath.

Couldn't have happened, she thought, choosing not even to consider her father's comments that she would have "assistance" in her studies.

She put that thought out of her head at once and looked at the first page of the book. It was covered with writing that at first appeared impossible to decipher. Antonia hadn't considered the fact that early nineteenth century handwriting would be so different from the current style. She knew it intellectually, having heard one of her professors mention it in a class on colonial literature, but she'd never experienced the reality of it before. As she stared at the words that made no sense to her, she thought that doing her research was going to be a lot harder and more time-consuming than she had thought.

Then something else happened, something even more astonishing than the book's opening by itself. The writing on the page seemed to quiver and become indistinct. It faded and almost disappeared. As Antonia watched, it began to darken once again, and as it did, the words flowed on the page and then resolved themselves into something that resembled modern handwriting. Antonia found that she could read it easily.

It was all just some trick of the lighting in here, she thought. *I could have read it all along if I'd only looked at it a little more carefully.*

Even as she told herself that, she knew it was a lie.

But a comforting lie is better than the truth in some situations. She looked at the page to see what was written there.

Even though the writing was now plain, there were some difficulties still remaining. For one thing, there were no dates as there would have been in a regular journal. Events were described one after the other, but there was no certainty, at least as far as Antonia was concerned, that they were recorded in chronological order, or any other kind of order.

Furthermore, there was no name associated with the writing. Antonia had hoped for a diary or similar book, for she knew that Americans had been great diarists right from the beginnings of colonial culture. Samuel Sewall, one of the judges during the Salem witch trials had kept a diary, as had Roger Byrd in Virginia, along with many others. Antonia had read portions of both men's writings in textbooks, and it was well arranged and dated, which gave it a certain authoritativeness that the book in front of her lacked.

Maybe she should start with another volume, she thought. Even though this was the one her father had selected for her, it was possible that he had simply pulled it from the shelves at random.

Antonia looked at the shelves and saw that there was a gap in about the middle of the first row of books. So Frederick hadn't taken the first book. Most likely he had just chosen one that looked interesting. Antonia would put this one back in its place and try another.

But when she tried to close the cover, she found that she couldn't.

She gave the book a push.

It didn't budge.

She shoved harder. The book might as well have been nailed to the table.

She stood up, put both hands under the book's cover, and strained to lift it. It moved as far as it would have if it had been made of ten layers of lead, which is to say it moved not at all.

Antonia sat back down in the folding chair and stared at the book. There was nothing unusual about it other than its age, or nothing that was visible to the eye. But something unseen was at work here, and Antonia didn't like it at all. She tapped her fingers rapidly on the table while she thought things over.

What it came down to was that the book in front of her hadn't been chosen randomly, even if her father thought it had. It was the book she was going to have to read, whether she wanted to read it or not. Either that, or she was going to have to give up the whole thing and pick another topic to write about for her Special Project.

As soon as she thought about making a change, the light in the attic dimmed and a light wind seemed to move through the place, raising the dust on the floor and causing the spider webs to sway and billow.

"All right," Antonia said aloud, trying to resolutely ignore the chill running down her spine. "I'll read the damned book."

The light brightened and the wind ceased. Antonia took the pencil in her hand and moved the pad within easy reach.

Then she looked down at the book and started to read.

CHAPTER EIGHT

There is a place that exists outside of time and space. No rational being would admit its existence, or contemplate its inhabitants.

Nevertheless it *does* exist. As do the beings that reside there.

They can, occasionally, move into what we refer to as *reality*, for their reality stretches across our own—a borderland unseen by most humans. Perhaps it reaches even other realities, though what those realities might be are unknown.

It is a dark and formless place, and the beings there do not look like anything at all that we would recognize as human. Not in our most forgiving definition of the term.

Nevertheless, the beings *are* there.

It is a place without sound, and therefore there is no speech among those who dwell there.

Nevertheless, they do speak, as did two of them who encountered one another there.

"So, Jonathan, you have become a problem to me yet again. You were ever a thorn in my side."

"I never tried to kill you, Thomas, and I never had others killed for my own pleasure and profit."

"Oh, it was no pleasure to me, Jonathan, though I cannot, of course, speak for McCool. I sometimes wonder what might have happened to McCool."

"He is, I believe, residing in somewhat warmer climes than these."

"There is no warmth here, brother of mine."

"Do not call me your brother, Thomas, for brother you never were to me."

"Oh, I was that, and more, Jonathan. Were not Cain and Abel brothers?"

"They were, and such a brother as Cain was to Abel, so were you to me. But you did not succeed in your aims, Thomas, though I died as Abel did."

"I never killed you, brother."

"No. You left that to your creature, McCool, and he did for me very well. You did not succeed with Agatha Derlicht, however, and the fire you hoped would destroy her destroyed nothing except your hopes."

"I was tricked and deceived. I believed, as did my father, that I was the thirteenth son."

"Even in the womb you strove for that distinction. In the end, your strivings proved futile, Thomas, as such strivings always will."

"I take your meaning, Jonathan, but this time you will not win. I will have what I want, and I will walk again in the world of living men. I will see the things that were denied me in my first life, and I will taste the joys of them."

"That can never be."

"You cannot stop me."

"I have already made a start."

"True, but only because I did not expect you. Mason is weak and unformed. I will win him over, by fear or by guile, and he will be the instrument of my return."

"I say it will not happen."

"And I say, 'Try to stop me.'"

"I shall do more than try, Thomas."

"We will see, brother of mine. We will see."

And then they were gone, if such a term can be applied to a place that exists out of space, and out of time.

CHAPTER NINE

T he human mind's ability to rationalize is a wonderful thing. By the time he had finished a bourbon and soda, Mason was convinced that everything he had experienced was nothing more than an extremely vivid dream. A dream induced by the stress he'd been putting on himself during the course of his research and his father's nagging to find a wife, and his threats to cut off the money supply. He'd simply fallen asleep in the chair.

Or perhaps Mason had disconnected from reality for a moment, during which time he had slipped out of his chair and fallen on the floor, hitting his head in the process and stunning himself. The rest was what he had dreamed or imagined before he had regained the complete use of his faculties. That was all there was to it. There was nothing preternatural or supernatural about it.

Mason was equally convinced that James's insistence on the reality of the "vision" was nothing more than James's own rationalization of events.

"Face it," Mason said, looking at his father over the rim of his heavy lead-crystal glass. "Our family has more power and prestige than a lot of families in New York, most of them in fact, but you don't think that's good enough. So you're clinging to some old family legend in the hope that we can get even more power and prestige."

James was sitting in an old wing chair that had been in Noir Manor for far longer than Mason had been alive. He held his glass wrapped in his long fingers and smiled as if he knew something that Mason did not.

"Sooner or later, you'll find out you're wrong," James said. "Not about what I want. You're right about that. But you'll come to see that you're wrong about what happened to you in the study and come to accept that it was more than you think. When I told you that something was stirring in Geiststadt, I wasn't making an idle comment. You'll come to see that I was correct. It will happen in time."

Mason didn't agree. He said, "I think my computers have all the power I need, and no one from the realm of the dead is going to take it from me."

James continued to smile. "I hope you're right about that last part, at least. By the way, have you been down to the workroom to check on things recently?"

The "workroom" was a well-hidden, nearly inaccessible chamber carved out of the native rock below the basement of Noir Manor. It had been created by Benjamin Noir for his own elaborate alchemical researches, and the Captain, as he was called by some, had spent many hours there in his attempts to convert base metal to gold, among his other many experiments. The space had been modernized since the Captain's time and now held things that old Benjamin would never have understood. However, while Mason was not trying to create gold, his work with MIND-NET had led him to experiment with certain things that were almost equally as outlandish.

"I go down there every day," Mason said. "It's the kind of thing you have to keep an eye on."

Indeed it was, for in the workroom Mason was delving into the realm of DNA computing. Nanotechnology had progressed to the point that DNA, combined with certain enzymes, could actually be used to store and process information, though the "computer" looked like nothing more than a test tube full of water.

Mason believed that in the future there might be autonomous bio-molecular computers that patrolled a person's body to monitor health and well being. If these nanocomputers could relay the proper information about the brain's electrical impulses, MIND-NET might be able to do all the things Mason hoped, and more besides.

He was hindered only by the fact that his family's wealth was not unlimited. He did not have any lab assistants to help him with his experiments, and he was sometimes pressed to buy and install the latest equipment. The field of DNA computing was so new, and advances were being made so rapidly, that Mason had trouble keeping up with what other, better-financed labs were doing, and he sometimes thought that he was losing ground instead of making the progress he hoped for.

But he sincerely believed in MIND-NET and its possibilities, and he wasn't going to let anything interfere if he could help it, especially not some crazy visions of dead people and ancient gods. Money, now, that was another matter entirely.

"I know you're careful," James said. "But with something so delicate as DNA and enzymes, you easily lose important work if anything untoward happened."

Mason drained the remains of his drink and set the glass down on the table beside his chair.

"You mean like a visit from a ghost?" he said.

"Whatever suits," James said.

"I don't think I have to worry about that. Nothing really happened up there in the study, no matter what you think, and there's no use in trying to convince me that it did. I was just overworked, worried too much about what we'd been talking about, and I stressed out. That's all it was."

"I don't want to stress you out," James said. "On the other hand, I was completely serious about your finding a wife. And the sooner the better. If the only way I can encourage you enough is to cut off your finances, then that's what I'll have to do. I'm not saying I'd like it."

Mason's face reddened with anger, but he forced himself to speak in a controlled voice.

"I can get private financing."

"Maybe that's true, but I doubt it. I know that your experiments are legitimate, but what you're planning as a result is not something that most private institutions would be willing to support. And you know it. Besides, you're too small an operation for them to have much faith in you."

Mason didn't trust himself to speak, but he knew James was right. He nodded his assent.

"So you'd better be thinking about devoting some of your time to finding a suitable wife," James continued.

"You're not bad looking, and you have a wealthy family. No matter how clumsy with women you think you are, you'll find someone. She doesn't have to be a movie star."

Mason's head was throbbing, and he was afraid he might have another little mental episode. He was glad there was no computer monitor around.

"Are you listening to me, Mason?" his father said.

"I'm listening," Mason answered in a strained voice.

"Good. As I said, I don't want you to feel stressed about this. After all, dating and marriage are perfectly normal activities and have been for a long time. Millions of people engage in them every day."

"I'm not millions of people."

"No. I'll grant you that. You are a Noir, and we are a unique family. We do, however, need one more member, by marriage, and your job is to find her. Soon."

Mason stood up. His legs were still a bit weak, but they carried him to the door without incident. When he reached it, he turned back and said, "I believe I'll go to the workroom for a while before dinner."

He had to make an effort to keep his voice level, but he wasn't certain he'd succeeded.

"A good idea," James said. "After what happened upstairs, you'll want to be sure all is in order there."

"Then I'll log on to some computer dating services," Mason said.

James chuckled. "Sarcasm doesn't become you, son. You're not very good at it."

Mason didn't reply. He left the room and passed through the hallway to the door that led to the basement.

As walked by an open door, his mother, Laura called to him.

Mason didn't really want to talk to her, but he stopped and went into the room, which was Noir Manor's library, as it had been ever since the house's construction. For some reason, however, most of Captain Noir's books had long since vanished from the shelves. More modern volumes had replaced them, some of which were quite valuable. Some members of the Noir family had always been great readers, a trait that Mason had inherited. He had grown up surrounded by all the classic tales from world literature, not to mention first editions of Hemingway and Faulkner, Hawthorne and Twain, Hammett and Chandler, Updike and Bellow. The books were not extremely valuable because they had been bought for reading, not collecting, and they had been handled frequently, by Mason and by others before him. Most of the dust jackets were tattered to one degree or another, and some of the books even had pages that were spotted by spilled food and drink.

Mason's mother didn't care about the condition of the books, however. She loved books for the words they contained, and she enjoyed re-reading the classics as well as adding contemporary volumes to the library.

The room itself had shelves on all four walls. The shelves started at the floor and went all the way up to the twelve-foot ceiling. The only breaks in the shelves were for the doorway and a large window that looked out into the back yard of the manor. A wheeled ladder that stood in one corner was used to climb within reach of the upper shelves. A heavy oak desk sat in the middle of the room, and a green-shaded banker's lamp sat on it.

Hardly anyone ever used the desk. There were two wing chairs, one of which was situated by the window. That was where anyone using the library usually chose to sit, as the light was good for reading, and the chair was comfortable.

Mason's mother smiled at him from that chair as he entered the room. She put a bookmark in John Ciardi's translation of Dante's *Comedy*, closed the book, and laid it in her lap.

Laura was not as thin as James, and her hair was light brown, not gray, though Mason knew that was due to her regular visits to the hairdresser. She was a twinkly sort, and Mason had always felt that she was a little out of place in Noir Manor, an edifice not noted for its twinkling.

"Judging from the expression on your face," Laura told him, "I'd say you and your father must have had a difficult discussion."

"And I'll bet you know all about it," Mason said, for he was well aware that his father and mother kept few secrets from each other.

"You're our son. Of course we talk about you and your prospects."

"I wish you wouldn't. I wish you'd just let me go my own way."

"You're living in our house, and we're supporting you. I believe we have a right to some say-so in you life."

As much as Mason hated to admit it, she had a point. After his graduation from college, she and James had encouraged him to move back home and continue his work there. They had told him they would provide him with whatever he needed, and they had kept that promise.

For the first time, however, he wondered if they had done it for him or for themselves. Odd that he had never thought of it that way before, but now it all at once seemed clear to him that they, or their idea of the Noir family destiny, were the reason he was there. They had provided for all his needs, but they had done so because not they were generous but because they wanted something from him.

He should have known it before, he thought. They had never been subtle about encouraging him to get out of the house, to meet people, to date some nice young woman. And up until now, they had been patient with his failure to do so.

Oh, he had tried, at first. He had met people, even women, and he had gone to movies and sporting events with friends, but he had never been comfortable around other people. He had preferred to work with his computers and his experiments, and with the passage of years, his orientation had become more and more inward. He left the house less and less often, and the friends that he had made eventually stopped calling.

Mason realized that he had become a virtual hermit. He had daily contact with his parents, and he was in touch with other people by e-mail, but those were scientists and computer experts, not friends. They were not really even acquaintances because he had never met them. He had no idea what they looked like, what books they read, what foods they enjoyed, what movies they watched.

For that matter, Mason had not been to a movie in an actual movie in a theater for years. He watched DVDs with his parents or alone, but James and Laura were the ones who chose the movies. Mason hadn't been to a video store since they'd replaced the VHS player years earlier.

"Jesus Christ," Mason said. "I'm the freaking Count of Monte Cristo."

"I wouldn't put it quite that way," Laura told him. "This isn't exactly the Chateau d'If, now, is it? And your grooming is much better than the count's was when he was incarcerated there, I believe."

"Having a good barber doesn't make me any less a prisoner," Mason said, "but I'm glad I still get out to get a haircut now and then."

That was about the only place he went, he thought. He didn't go to the supermarket or the drugstore, the theater or the football stadium.

"I know," Laura said, "and that's becoming a problem. Your father and I had hoped that you would be married by now, but we also realized the importance of your work. We thought you might be able to do it and maintain some semblance of a social life, but that hasn't happened. There has to be a change."

"I've already heard this lecture," Mason said.

He didn't want to get angry with his mother, and he hoped the conversation would come to an end before he did.

"Well, I hope you've taken what your father said to heart."

"I have," Mason said.

"And I hope you'll act on it."

"I will," Mason said. "I promise."

"That's good to hear. I know you won't have any trouble finding someone. You're a fine young man."

Mason might have had something to say to that, but Laura opened her book and ran her finger down the page as if looking for the line where she had stopped reading. Mason looked past her, out the window, at the remains of Captain Benjamin's "glass house."

This had once been the largest structure in Geiststadt, according to James. Protected by a slight depression, and by Noir Manor itself from storms, yet exposed on all sides to the sun, it had been huge, a hundred feet long and three stories high. In it, Benjamin Noir had conducted more of his experiments, though exactly what kind of plants he had grown there, Mason was not sure.

The glass house was gone now, the many windows having been broken or used in other structures in the town. All that remained was a bit of the stone foundation and north wall, and the ruin of the great furnace that had heated the water that ran beneath it through ceramic pipes. The pipes, or what was left of them were probably still there, Mason thought, covered by the soil.

He realized that he and the Captain were not so very different in one way. They were both experimenters, both looking for something beyond the ordinary. If the Captain had chosen to search in unconventional ways, so too did Mason, but there the similarity ended. Mason's beliefs did not extend beyond the real world as he could perceive it, while the Captain's were rumored to have extended well beyond any reality Mason could—or wanted—to perceive. Mason wanted solid proof for everything, and he had no desire to tap into any powers other than those of rational science.

Laura looked up from her book.

"Was there something else you wanted to say?" she asked.

"No. I was just thinking about the Captain and all that must have gone on in this house."

"He was a great man, but he didn't realize his dreams. His sons let him down."

"I can take a hint," Mason said.

Laura smiled. "I'm sure you can, but it wasn't a hint. It was just a statement of fact. Your father and I have a great deal of faith in you, and we know you won't make the same mistakes that some of your ancestors did."

"Thanks," Mason said. If messing around with the supernatural was a mistake, they could be sure he wasn't going to make it. "I'm going down to the workroom for a while."

But Laura was already lost in her book again, treading the circles of hell with Dante Alighieri.

CHAPTER TEN

A ntonia brushed a stray lock of hair away from her face and looked at her watch in amazement. Could it really be that four hours had passed since she had started reading the old leather book in her attic?

Her head was spinning with all the things she had read and the secrets she had learned, and she wondered if they were all true.

But why shouldn't they be? she asked herself. *Who would have taken the time to write those accounts if they weren't a record of actual events?*

She could hardly decide which of the tales she'd discovered was the most amazing. The book had begun with the real story of the head-taker, and now she knew the true origins of the frightening urban legend that had kept her awake and wide-eyed on more than one muggy summer night of her childhood. The legend was clearly based on a series of gory killings that had occurred in Geiststadt during the time when the Noirs and Derlichts had first settled there. While no heads had been taken, the murders were quite gruesome. Thomas Noir was responsible, though he had not committed the actual murders.

Even more amazing, Washington Irving had been involved, seemingly because of the resemblance of the murders to the story he had told of the Headless Horseman. Irving had come to Geiststadt to investigate, and had learned about Thomas's part in the killings. Shortly after that time, Irving had left America to live abroad, possibly because he feared that Thomas might somehow retaliate against him because of his knowledge.

Antonia was certain that this one discovery alone would make her Special Project one of the best and most original ever to have been written at NYU. She was also sure that Dr. Martin would be quite impressed by what she had learned.

He would no doubt want her to find corroborating evidence if possible, but even if she could not, this written account, unquestionably authentic, would be enough to cause quite a commotion in the usually sedate world of early American literary studies. At the very least, it would bring new prominence to Washington Irving, ignite renewed interest in his life and work, and provide fodder for journal articles and academic arguments for years to come.

But there had been much more in the dusty old leather-bound. True, the rest was likely to be of more interest to Antonia's family than to literary scholars, but what she had found was fascinating.

One thing she had read was the dark, sad tale of Thomas and Jonathan Noir, twin brothers who were remarkably different in appearance, temperament, and character. Again, she had only the book in front of her to rely on, but the narrative was very convincing. If what she read was true, and she believed that it was, Thomas was responsible not only for Jonathan Noir's death but for the destruction by fire of the first Derlicht Haus. And it seemed that Jonathan Noir had somehow saved Agatha Derlicht from the flames.

Antonia wondered why her father had never told her about these connections. For that matter, why had he never read the old books himself? Or if he had read them, why hadn't he given her some hint of what she was going to find in them?

She had so many questions that she had written a number of them down on her yellow pad to help her remember what they were. Some of them couldn't be answered by her father, of course, but others could.

However, those questions were only the beginning, for Antonia had read other things on the book's yellowing pages as well. There were veiled references to ancient prophecies that claimed a strange bond between the Derlicht and Noir families. It seemed that the destinies of the two families were inextricably intertwined and had been so before either of them had settled in America.

And even though she had uncovered these things and more, Antonia had not yet reached the end of the book. She was eager to see what else she might find, but she was tired and hungry and quite curious to hear what her father would have to say about her notes and her questions.

Antonia pushed herself back from the table, the chair legs scraping across the wooden flooring like metal claws. She stood up and stretched her arms toward the ceiling to get the kinks out of her body. She felt she'd done enough studying for one day, and it was in her mind to call it quits, when a cold chill passed across the room, swirled about her ankles and ran up the back of her legs like icy, skeletal fingers.

She looked around the empty room. Nothing but silence and dust and spider webs. *My imagination*, Antonia thought, then felt the fingers again—but this time they weren't running lightly along the back of her legs. This time they were claws, ice-coated talons digging into her flesh.

Antonia gasped at the painful sensation. "What?" she managed to gasp.

The claws worked their way upwards, ending at the base of her skull, piercing her deep inside. Antonia tried to scream, could see her breath steaming in the chill air, but could barely rasp out a breath. Her knees buckled, the pain was excruciatingly sharp—a migraine buried in the bottom of her brain. Dark spots wandered across her field of vision.

Seconds before she lost consciousness, she heard the voice. A sharp whipping whisper. "You'll finish when *I* say you're done!"

Then the darkness took her completely.

Spider webs. Antonia pried open her eyes, and groaned. *What the hell happened?* she wondered. The last thing she could clearly remember was standing up to go downstairs for a break, feeling an icy sensation, and then...nothing. The dim light of the attic illuminated the spider webs hanging above her, and Antonia realized with a start that she was lying on the floor. She struggled to her feet. Dirt and dust still covered every surface other than those of the table and chair. *How long was I out?* She checked her watch. *More than an hour.*

Stretching again, Antonia tried to make sense of things. Perhaps she'd grown too consumed by her interest in the book and its contents, stood too fast, and gotten what was commonly called a "head rush". She wouldn't have been the first person who'd passed out from the dizzying sensation—when she'd been a kid, causing them on purpose had been a passing fad. Still, she'd never heard of anyone passing out for an hour or more either.

Antonia shook her head. "I'm just tired," she said to herself, stretching again. She yawned, picked up her pad and pencil, and reached out to close the book, then hesitated. There was something odd going on, she decided, but what it was escaped her. She looked at the book again, and realized what it was.

Before she'd passed out, she was only a third the way through the volume, but now...Antonia felt confident that she knew the details of the entire thing. And that just wasn't possible. She began turning the pages, faster and faster, knowing what each would say before she saw it. With a mixed feeling of horror and wonder, she slammed the cover shut—this time it didn't resist her at all. Perhaps its failure to do so signaled that she had learned enough for one day to satisfy her unseen "assistant".

She looked at her pad and pencil. The pencil tip was worn down to a dull nub, and the pages were filled with notes in a handwriting that bore little resemblance to her own.

"What the hell is going on here?" Antonia wondered aloud, then shook her head. Her father had some explaining to do. She replaced the book on the shelf, turned off the light, and went downstairs to get some answers.

"Now *that* I can't explain," Fredrick was telling her. "Perhaps you got caught up in your reading and got further along than you thought."

"The *whole* book?" Antonia asked. "I think I'd have noticed. And how do you explain that the handwriting isn't mine?"

Fredrick shrugged. "I can't," he said. "Not in any way you'd want to believe."

"Try me," Antonia said.

"Very well," Fredrick answered. "The next time you're in the attic, compare the notes on your pad to the handwriting in the books."

"Why?" she asked.

"I think you'll find them quite similar," Fredrick said. "Very similar indeed."

Antonia thought for a moment, then nodded. "Agatha wrote those books, didn't she?"

"Many of them, yes," he said. "My theory is that you've experienced some form of automatic writing."

Antonia had heard of automatic writing—it occurred

when a person channeled the spirit of the dead and acted as the medium for them to write messages from the next world.

"Automatic writing, huh?" she asked. "That doesn't...feel quite right."

"I'm sure it will become clear in time."

Another thought occurred to her. "How come you've never read the books?"

"I never read them because I couldn't," Frederick told her when she questioned him about it. "I have opened them many times, but all I could make out was some kind of strange writing on the page. It never meant anything to me, no matter how much or how long I looked at it. It was nothing but brown, faded squiggles. I was hoping it might someday make itself plain to the right person. I'm glad you were the one."

"What if I hadn't been?" Antonia wanted to know.

They were in the kitchen again, and Antonia was eating a chicken salad sandwich that her father had prepared for her. It was on whole-wheat bread with a thick slice of tomato and some lettuce.

"If you hadn't been the right one, I would have had to try again with someone else," Frederick said. "One of your sisters, perhaps. But I didn't think I would have to do that. I was sure you would be the one to whom the book would reveal itself. You have the temperament and the devotion of a scholar, and you are the thirteenth daughter of a Derlicht. The book was waiting for you."

Antonia almost believed him. So many odd things had

happened in such a short time that she was ready to believe almost anything at all.

She took a bite of her sandwich and chewed it
thoughtfully. When she had swallowed, she said, "So
you didn't know the story of Thomas and Jonathan
Noir?"

"Only the vague outlines. And I have never been sure
about what happened to the first Derlicht Haus. I knew
that it had burned, of course, and that the attic had
somehow survived. I did not know Jonathan's or
Thomas's part in that event, nor did I know that
Jonathan had been the savior of Agatha Derlicht. I am
as surprised as you are to find that a Noir actually saved
a member of our family. It doesn't seem all that likely."

Antonia finished her sandwich, pushed the plate away,
and had a drink of milk.

"And all those old prophecies?" she said.

"I knew them only from vague hints and stories passed
down through the family. Along with the story of Thomas
and Jonathan, they would seem to explain some of the
enmity—the rivalry that I mentioned—between our family
and the Noirs. They also help explain how the Noirs have
held onto their power in this state for so many years."

Antonia didn't understand how the stories did that,
although they did make it clear that the Derlichts had
once been the equal of the Noirs, or even their superiors.
And they showed that the decline of the Derlichts had
begun with the destruction of the original Derlicht Haus.

Antonia thought for a moment about Poe's story "The
Fall of the House of Usher," which she had read many

times and discussed in more than one of her classes at NYU. In that tale, the house and the family had been so closely connected that the destruction of one meant the destruction of the other. Could houses and humans really have had that kind of bond at one time, a bond achieved by some kind of magical means? It seemed obvious from her reading that magic of one kind or another, maybe of several kinds, had entered into the Noirs' seizing of power. And that the magic had something to do with Benjamin Noir.

She looked down at her legal pad and flipped through the pages of notes. Yes. There it was. A mention of Benjamin Noir's sea voyages and the things he had learned in the lands he had visited. He had brought back with him many strange and unusual things, including a knowledge of the occult, the idols of other religions, and maybe even a few spells and incantations. He had also brought with him to Geiststadt a woman named Callie, who had been the family servant and who had possessed magical powers of her own.

So maybe Frederick was right, after all. The stories in the old books did explain how the Noirs had gained and held their power, and it had to do with magic and the occult and psychic abilities.

Antonia had to ask for some clarification, however. She said, "Do you mean to say you believe that the Noirs are still using magic?"

Frederick gave her an affectionate grin.

"No," he said. "But I believe some vestige of the power that the old sea captain Benjamin Noir discovered still clings to them and gives them an advantage over others, whether they are aware of it or not. And they well may not be. I also believe that any power that our family had was somehow stripped away from us by that fire or its aftermath."

"Well," Antonia said, "I've learned a lot more than I ever thought I would, and I've only just begun to research in those books we have. I wonder if I should go back up and read some more."

Frederick looked out the kitchen window. The shadows were gathering around Derlicht Haus, and a dark wind was moving in the trees.

"I think you've learned enough for one day," he said. "Why not put your notes in order and see if they tell you anything more?"

"There's one thing they won't tell me," Antonia said. "And it's something I'd like to know. Maybe it's there and I just haven't seen it yet."

"What is that?"

"Why did Agatha write everything down so that no one else could read it?

"I don't think you have to be concerned about that," Frederick said. "The book may have simply been waiting for the right time and the right person to reveal its contents."

Antonia was about to protest the impossibility of what her father was saying, but then she remembered how the book itself had resisted her. Perhaps her father was right. The book had a mind of its own, and if it wanted to be read, then it would be—but not until.

The scholar in her mind, her logical, learned brain was screaming, "No! No!", but the sounds of that voice were rapidly fading away.

"I suppose," she said, "that we'll never know."

"I'm certain you're right, Antonia," her father said.

She turned her attention to her notes, so didn't hear his last, mumbled comment.

"I pray that you're right," he said, "for your sake."

CHAPTER ELEVEN

The workroom hidden deep beneath Noir Manor had once been almost cave-like, but that had long since changed. Now the once rough-hewn walls were smooth and white, the room itself soundproofed, the temperature made comfortable by a laboratory quality air-conditioning and heating system. Non-glare lighting was utilized to provide quality illumination with a minimum of eyestrain. The entire room was kept spotlessly clean, and one part of it had been walled off with glass. Inside that area, which Mason used for his lab work, everything was as sterile as could be managed.

Mason never went inside it without wearing a lab suit that he kept in a special cleaning chamber, where it was sterilized after every wearing and kept that way.

A few trinkets from the Captain's time still remained, locked away and forgotten in the drawers of the wooden cabinets that lined the walls. Mason was aware of these small items, including some odd carvings from Africa and something that looked as if it might be a wand, but they held little interest for him. While the Captain had been dabbling in what Mason would have ridiculed as mere pseudo-science, Mason would have been insulted if anyone had questioned the value of what he was attempting.

He would have had to admit, however, in his more honest moments, that anyone who was told that the lab contained the latest in computer technology would have laughed out loud. There was nothing in sight that even resembled a conventional computer. The place looked more like the lab of a mad scientist from an old black-and-white horror movie than a place where computers were being created by chemical means.

Now Mason stood in the doorway and looked things over. Everything seemed to be in order. *Not*, he reminded himself, *that there had been any reason to expect otherwise*. If his father wanted to believe in ghostly apparitions who might somehow get into the workroom, that was fine with Mason, but he wasn't going to let himself fall for that sort of thing.

But even as the thought that, a vague feeling of unease came over him. He walked around the room, checking his notebooks, making sure that everything was where it belonged. But his worry wasn't justified. Nothing had been touched; nothing was out of place.

He looked through the glass walls into the sterile lab environment. One table held a state-of-the-art computer system that he used to run the computations and analysis side of his masterwork: the clear vials that held his experimental DNA computers. Filled with a saline and glucose mix, they provided the perfect medium for his current experiment—trying to predict the movement of cells outside the regulated system of the human body. If he could that, then introducing a new "cell" or miniaturized computer that was directed might have some hope of working. Otherwise, the new "cell" would be attacked by the other cells as a foreign body.

The vials were exactly as he had left them, and he laughed at himself for having worried. Nothing was going to happen to them. *Still*, he thought, *it couldn't hurt anything to step into his lab suit and double check.*

Mason stepped into the cleaning chamber and pulled on his lab suit, then stepped through another door that led directly into the lab. As he walked around the table, his sense of unease returned, though it took several moments for him to realize why.

His computer system was running.

And he knew for a fact that it had been in standby mode when he left it.

The screen flared in blues and greens, words appearing and disappearing faster than he could make them out. If he hadn't known better, he would have said it was some kind of system fault. "What the hell?" he wondered aloud, as he approached the system.

He reached out to shut it down, when it flared once again, painfully bright, and the screen went black momentarily, and then the words appeared in bright, blue letters:

BRING ME BACK!

"No," Mason said, his voice just barely audible. "No."

BRING ME BACK!

"Who are you?" Mason asked. "What do you want?"

He could feel his knees shaking, and the tugging sensation he'd experienced upstairs in the study was returning. "No," he repeated. The computer made a faint buzzing sound, and on the screen a swirl of blues and reds appeared in a vaguely hypnotic, rotating pattern, before being replaced with more words:

BRING ME BACK! BRING ME BACK!
THOMAS NOIR LIVES! THOMAS NOIR LIVES!
BRING ME BACK! BRING ME BACK!

The words were repeated over and over across the screen. Mason felt cold sweats break out on his brow, and the sensation of being tugged grew stronger, even as he felt himself falling forward. He tried to catch himself on the table, missed, felt his head rushing toward the table top and knew he was going to hit it and then...nothing.

There was sand in his mouth—gritty and hot and tasting of ash. Mason tried to spit and found he didn't have enough saliva to manage it. His head ached and he groaned as he tried to push himself to his feet.

"Each year, humans grow softer and weaker," a familiar voice said behind him.

Mason grunted in surprise and turned over. "Thomas," he said. "Right?"

"As rain after sundown," Thomas replied. "Let me help you up." He reached out a hand, which Mason recoiled from.

"I'll manage," Mason said. "Thanks."

"You're being silly," Thomas said. But he didn't offer the hand again.

Mason struggled to his feet. "My father says you're real."

Thomas nodded. "Of course. Your father is a wise man. He doesn't have much *heka* himself, in fact, he's weak in all kinds of ways, but he knows enough to know I'm very real." He paused, then added. "I may be even more real than you are, Mason Noir."

Mason shrugged. "I doubt it," he said. "Even if you are real, which I doubt, you're nothing more than a phantom." He looked around the desert landscape. "This place, too, is nothing more than illusion. A dream."

"A dream? A phantom?" Thomas asked, his voice mocking. "Is the bruise on your chest from where I hit you earlier a dream? The sand caught in the laces of your shoes? The sweat you feel on your skin from the heat of this wasteland?" He shook his head. "No, Mason. It's no dream, and I am no phantom."

In the distance, a dog-like yapping sound could be heard, and Mason struggled to suppress a shudder. Dealing with Thomas was one thing, but Anubis was quite another. "Suppose for the moment," Mason said, turning his attention back to Thomas, "that I accept that you are real. What do you want from me?"

"Just what you read on your machine. I want you to bring me back." Thomas laughed. "The very life and death decision of which we spoke when we last met here."

"Bring you back?" Mason asked. "But if you're real, what do you need me for?"

"Ahhh," said Thomas, "that's the difficult part. I am real, but I'm also not."

"I don't understand," Mason said.

"In this place, I am real," Thomas said. "I can touch you, you can touch me, all the normal rules apply and then some. But beyond this place... in your reality, if you will, I am a spirit. Sometimes I can have an effect on inanimate objects, such as your machine, and even on people—if they are susceptible to it—but what I can't have is life. I can feel *nothing*."

"So what does that have to do with me?"

"Everything!" Thomas said. "While I can't claim to understand your machines or your experiments, I have heard you talk with your father about your goals: eternal life, new bodies for the sick or the dying..."

"You want to use MIND-NET to come back into a new body?" Mason asked.

"Yes!" Thomas said. "That's exactly right."

Mason couldn't help himself. He tried to hold it in, but the laughter got away from him, and before he knew it he was laughing so hard his stomach hurt.

"What do you find so amusing, kinsman?" Thomas asked, his voice tight.

"I'm sorry," Mason said, struggling to get his laughter under control, "but you really *don't* understand at all. I'm years from being able to use MIND-NET in any practical way. *Years.* And maybe never. It might not work at all. And it was intended for use by living beings. Even if I could use it that way now—and I can't—there's not enough DNA of yours left to even begin the process of growing you a new body."

Thomas looked at Mason for a long, silent moment, and under the intensity of that gaze, Mason felt himself wilt, the laughter running from his body like air from a deflating balloon. "It is you that does not understand," Thomas said. "I have *years*. Time has no meaning here."

"But it does for me," Mason said. "I'll likely be an old man before MIND-NET is ready for use."

"You must work faster then," Thomas said. "I have waited a long time, and I have time, and will wait some more, but my patience is not infinite." He pointed a finger at Mason. "You must use all the resources at your disposal to speed your work."

Mason shook his head. "This isn't something that can be rushed," he said. "Besides, why in the world would I want to bring you back to life? From all I've heard, you were a recluse when you were alive, and there are other stories as well. Dark stories."

"You will bring me back, Mason," Thomas said, "or you will suffer the consequences."

"Are you threatening me?"

"I do not threaten," Thomas said.

Mason looked at the wasteland around him. In the distance, heat spirals rose up towards a blood-colored sky. "I don't think so," Mason said. "You're not my father, you're not anything, and I won't be ordered around by a long-dead spirit with a bad attitude."

"Perhaps an object lesson will help you along a better path," Thomas said, then sprang forward, swinging his arms downward in a chopping motion that caught Mason's upraised arms and knocked them out of the way.

94

He followed this with a sharp uppercut to the ribs that took Mason's breath away.

He stumbled backward, trying to regain his footing and put some distance between them, but Thomas pressed his advantage, throwing feints and jabs that Mason tried vainly to block. Thomas was a large man, with an good reach, and when he did connect with a solid punch to Mason's jaw, it felt like the blow of a sledgehammer. Mason's head snapped back, and he fell to his knees.

"This is the first lesson, Mason," Thomas said. "The second one will be worse."

On the ground, Mason shook his head to clear it, and wiggled his jaw back and forth. Seething in rage, he looked up at Thomas and got painfully to his feet. "Who said the first lesson was over, *kinsman*?" Mason asked, swinging a roundhouse blow that caught Thomas by surprise. The feel of his fist connecting was pure pleasure, and Thomas went down to one knee. Mason immediately tried to follow through with a kick to the face, but Thomas was agile and tricky, and he caught Mason's foot and twisted it aside.

Mason tried to roll with it, but ended up on the ground with Thomas standing over him, holding his foot and ankle in an excruciatingly tight grip. "Not I," Thomas said. Then he leaned forward, increasing the pressure on Mason's ankle until he thought sure it would snap.

He groaned in pain. "Enough!" Mason said.

"Nowhere near enough," Thomas replied. Then he leaned over Mason's face and spit on him.

The spit traveled in slow motion through the air, transforming itself as it fell, so that by the time it landed on Mason's chest, it was a large, hairy spider. It scuttled forward on legs the size of pencils. This close, Mason could see the poison dripping off the mandibles. He tried to wiggle away, but Thomas twisted his leg again. "I don't think so, Mason," he said. "Do you like my pet?"

"It's... it's *disgusting*," Mason choked out past the pain.

"She's beautiful," Thomas said, feigning hurt. "And oh so deadly. Shall I leave you to her, Mason? Shall I let go of your leg, and see if you can move fast enough to avoid her fangs?"

Mason shook his head, trying to keep his eyes on the spider that was now only an inch or two from his face.

"Perhaps I should send her to you late one night as you lay dreaming in your comfortable bed?"

"No," Mason said. "No."

"Good, then you'll agree to speed up your efforts and bring me back at the first opportunity?"

Through gritted teeth, Mason said, "Yes, anything."

"Excellent," Thomas said. "Most acceptable." He released Mason's leg, which was throbbing in time to his racing heartbeat.

"Now get that *thing* off me," Mason said.

"Of course," Thomas said, "she's only a little spit, you know." He reached out and covered the spider with his hand, when he lifted it, only a wet patch of spittle remained on Mason's shirt.

Mason breathed a sigh of relief and got shakily to his feet.

"Don't forget," Thomas said, "that this was a lesson. I can do much worse should you not meet my expectations."

"I won't forget," Mason said. "Now just let me wake up."

Thomas grinned, and in the distance, the yapping sound grew louder. "It's no dream, Mason. I am no dream. Now get to work!" He shoved Mason backward, and as Mason fell, he knew he was going through the tunnel again, spiraling past water and the laughing faces of forgotten gods. A blinding flash of light, red, then white, and something slammed into Mason's head hard enough to make him see stars just before the darkness took him.

The floor of the lab. Spotlessly clean and white. Mason blinked his eyes, trying to figure out if he had the strength to stand. He groaned at the pain in his head, his jaw, even his chest hurt. "This is out of control," he gritted, as he pulled himself to his feet by the edge of the table.

Standing, he took several deep breaths, while he gingerly probed his scalp. Sure enough, there was a nasty goose egg on his forehead from where he'd hit the table on his way down. And some swelling in his jaw.

"I need help," Mason said. "This can't be happening." He looked at the computer monitor. The system was shut off now, the screen a harmless black void. If his encounters with Thomas were real, then the world wasn't what he'd thought. If they weren't, he needed psychiatric help—before these episodes ended up killing him.

But they must be real, Mason's logical mind said. Look at the evidence.

"I've got to get out of here, got to think," Mason said

aloud. "I'm working too hard, and the possibility that James might take my funding away has...it's unhinged me."

If that happened, Mason would have no real reason for existing. He had devoted his life to this lab and to the computer work he was doing upstairs in the study. He had nothing else.

He slumped down on a stool and thought about what a sad commentary on his life that was. Beyond that lab and his more conventional computers, there was nothing to him. He recalled some of the people he had considered to be his friends in the past, realizing that it had been years since he had seen or talked to any of them.

Mason had read "The Fall of the House of Usher," and he thought now of the mad Roderick and his prematurely entombed sister. Neither of them had been able to leave their decaying family mansion because of their odd and debilitating illnesses. In the end, they had destroyed one another and brought the house crashing down around them in their death throes.

Jesus, he thought, *first I was the Count of Monte Cristo, and now I'm Roderick Usher. James is right. I really do need to get out more. If I don't this place is going to make me completely nuts. If it hasn't already.*

He wondered, however, if he could go out even if he wanted to. He remembered a biography of Nathaniel Hawthorne that he had read years ago. Hawthorne's mother had shut herself up in a room and withdrawn from the world after the death of her husband, and young Nathaniel had adopted her solitary ways. For most of the rest of his life, he had kept to himself, shutting himself away from the life of the towns he lived in. But he did get out occasionally, Mason remembered, and later in life he had actually gotten married.

If he could do it, so could I, Mason thought, but he didn't even know how to get started.

He ran a hand over his hair. It was getting a little long and could do with a trim, so maybe that would be the first step. He'd get a haircut, and instead of going right back home, he'd go somewhere else, to the movies, maybe, or to the mall. He could sit on a bench and watch people walk past him.

He found that just the thought of doing something like that made him nervous, and he started to perspire, though the room was quite cool.

Agoraphobia. The word popped into his mind. The fear of being in public places. He must have read about it in some psych book in college. But that couldn't be his problem. He wasn't afraid to go get his hair trimmed, and he wasn't afraid to go out onto the grounds around Noir Manor, so he wasn't afraid to leave home or go outside by himself.

On the other hand, he admitted to himself that he didn't like it, not one bit. Well, he was going to do something about it. He didn't know just what, but he was going to take action before he started to develop some of Roderick Usher's other, more debilitating, symptoms.

He got off the stool and left the workroom. When he got back upstairs, his mother was still in the library. He told her that he was going out for a while, but paused when her eyes widened at the sight of him.

"Are you all right?" she asked.

Mason shrugged. "I think so," he said. "Why?"

"You look like something that cat dragged in and threw up," she said, "not to put too fine a point on it."

Mason crossed the room to where a small window offered his reflection. She was right. His hair stood in corkscrews, his lab suit—which he'd not bother to take off—was rumpled and dirty with sand and sweat. His jaw was discolored and swollen. "You're right," he said. "I have looked better."

"I'll say," she added. "You're working too hard."

"Don't I know it?" Mason asked. He pulled off the lab suit. "Mind if I leave this here? I'll pick it up when I come back."

"Go right ahead," she said. "Are you sure you're all right?"

Mason nodded. "I hope so," he said.

She shut her book, keeping a finger in it to hold her place, and looked at him quizzically.

"You don't go out very often, Mason."

"I don't go out at all," he said. "Not in a long time, anyway. That's the problem. I've become a recluse. I need some fresh air for a change."

"It will do you good, I'm sure. I'm glad to see you taking this step, Mason. Are you going to meet anyone?"

"Not this time. I'm not sure anyone I used to know would meet me if I asked them to. Unlike me, all of them probably have actual lives, and I'm not part of them. I doubt if any of them even remember me."

"You might be surprised."

"I don't think so. I was never very close to anybody."

As he spoke the words, Mason realized how true the statement was. He had associated with people, gone places with them, had a few laughs now and then, but he had never shared himself with them, never told them the way he felt about things or shared any of his secrets. And, he knew now, they had never told him any of theirs, either. He wasn't sure that kind of relationship was even possible for him, but he was going to find out. Not to get his father's money, either, but to prove to himself that he was human.

"When will you be back?" Laura asked.

"I don't know," Mason said.

"Try to be careful, Mason," his mother said, turning her attention back to her novel. "The harshest lessons are usually taught to those not paying attention to the world around them."

The streets of Geiststadt were not crowded, but there were plenty of people around. Mason found that being out wasn't as bad as he had feared, but it wasn't an experience he would describe as pleasant. He didn't like the smell of automobile exhaust, or the noise the cars made, or the chatter of people who walked past him. On the other hand, the chill in the air felt unaccountably good, and he found that he enjoyed walking along with his hands in the pockets of his jacket, feeling almost as if he were a part of things instead of just some detached observer.

He walked along the main road that ran in front of Noir Manor. He passed insurance offices, a supermarket that he'd never entered, a bank, a drugstore. Everyone in town, he knew, was familiar with all those places, but he wasn't. He knew nothing about them or the people who owned them. Some of the people he passed on the street nodded and smiled as they passed him, and Mason's first tendency was to hunch down in his jacket and ignore them, but he tried to respond in kind. He wasn't very good at human contact, but he promised himself that he was going to change that.

Mason kept going until he came to the old Mill Pond. There was no longer a mill anywhere around, of course, and Mason wasn't sure how long it had been since one had stood somewhere nearby. In fact, he wasn't sure there had ever been a mill at all, though there must have been one back in the days when the town was first settled. People needed bread.

A couple of ducks swam on the pond, and a small boy and his mother were watching them.

"I want dem docks," the boy said.

"Ducks, dear," his mother said.

She was younger than Mason by at least ten years, yet she had already started a family. There would be someone in later years to cherish her memory and to talk about her to another generation. Maybe the boy would even remember the ducks he had seen on the Mill Pond on a cold day in winter.

"Docks," the boy said, pointing at the birds as they floated on the water. "I want dem docks."

"They don't belong to us," his mother told him. "We can't take them home, but we can come to see them any time we feel like it."

That simple statement of fact hit home with Mason.

They could come there wherever they cared to, and so could he. There was no reason he had to be a prisoner in his own house. He was as free as anyone to come and go as he pleased.

He never even stopped to wonder if these thoughts were his own, or if they had been implanted by James's suggestions, or if they might have come from some other source, some source much more sinister than any of the others. And he wouldn't have believed it possible even if he had. He was enjoying the sense of his own freedom too much to question it, and he made himself a promise that he would get out for a walk every day. If he happened to meet someone to talk to, all the better, though it wasn't necessary. Just getting out would be enough.

What could be the harm in that? he asked himself.

No harm at all, was the answer he gave.

It was on his way back to Noir Manor that Mason began to develop an intense feeling of discomfort. He didn't know why. He had surprised himself by being at ease during his little outing up until this point, but now something had changed.

It wasn't the weather. The day was still chill, and the wind was blowing no more and no less than it had been earlier.

There were no more people on the street, and if the traffic had increased, it had not increased by enough to make a pedestrian uncomfortable.

Perhaps it was a bit darker than it had been earlier, but that was nothing more than a thickening of the clouds. A perfectly ordinary meteorological event, Mason told himself, that's all.

He looked around to see if there was something odd going on.

There wasn't, or at least there was nothing that he could put a finger on.

No one rushed out of the bank waving a gun and carrying a bag of money.

No one tried to set fire to the insurance agency, and no one was shooting at the ducks on the Mill Pond.

But still there was something...

Then Mason caught a glimpse of something out of the corner of his eye and turned to look at an alleyway where there was a hint of motion.

It was nothing more than a blur, or less than that. All he saw was the corner of a gray Dumpster with a brown cardboard box sticking up over the edge, but he was sure that there had been something else there only a moment before. If there had been, however, now it was gone. Mason walked to the mouth of the alley and looked down it.

He didn't see anything unusual. There was the Dumpster, smelling of garbage. A little rill of water that came from no discernable source ran down the middle of the alley. A rusty fire escape clung to the side of one building. A piece of newspaper rustled along for a foot or two, pushed by the wind.

I'm just feeling jumpy because I never get out of the house, Mason thought. *Or*, his mind added, *because I'm being haunted—hunted?—by violent ancestors who are supposed to be dead.*

He turned back to the street just in time to see someone duck into the doorway of the drugstore.

He walked rapidly down the sidewalk, brushing past people without looking at them, hardly even aware that they were there. When he reached the drugstore, he looked into the doorway. No one was standing in it, and there didn't appear to be anyone in the drugstore, either, except for a bored cashier who was filing her fingernails and looking as if she hadn't seen a customer in the last few hours.

Mason looked all around him. He saw a street with a few people on their way here or there, but none of them appeared interested in him.

I'm losing it, he told himself. *Time to get back where I belong.*

He started toward home again. When he passed the Mill Pond, the woman and her little boy were gone, but there was a man standing on the other side of the water, a fair-haired man who looked strangely out of place.

Mason stared at the man and realized why he looked so odd. He was wearing clothing just like Thomas Noirs.

Stop it! Mason ordered himself. *Thomas is a ...*

The man raised a hand and waved at Mason, motioning him to come around to the other side of the pond, something that Mason had no intention of doing. Instead, he turned back to the sidewalk, looked this way and that, and then broke into a run. Within three steps he was running at full speed, running for the shelter of Noir Manor.

CHAPTER TWELVE

T he next day Antonia was up early. She couldn't wait to get back to work, though she was still somewhat troubled by the events of yesterday. She ate a piece of dry toast and drank some orange juice and then hurried to the attic, where she bent over the leather-bound book. She ignored the dust, dirt, and spiders, reading with fierce concentration, only stopping now and then to write a few notes in pencil on her yellow pad.

After about an hour, she read something that brought her up short. She sat up straight and put the pencil down beside the pad. Then she read the lines again, just to be sure she hadn't made a mistake.

She hadn't. They still said the same thing: "Power ever clings to power, and the power of one family is never lost entire. Though it may seem to have vanished, that power can be regained if the thirteenth daughter of the one should marry the thirteenth son of the other."

Antonia leaned back in her chair. It didn't take much figuring, even for one who had little sense of family history, to arrive at certain conclusions. The last sentence alone was why her father had wanted her to be the one to read the book. It probably also explained why the incomprehensible squiggles in the book had resolved themselves into readable words when she looked at them.

She, Antonia Derlicht, was the thirteenth daughter of the current generation of Derlichts.

As she reached for the pencil again, her fingers trembled, and she knocked the pencil to the floor. She ducked down to pick it up and saw a large black spider dangling from a sticky cord only a few inches from her face.

She recoiled in horror, and the spider dropped to the floor and scuttled along the base of the wall before disappearing.

It was almost as if the spider had been spying on her, Antonia thought.

Or was it just a spider? The light blonde hairs on Antonia's arms prickled. She grabbed the pencil and straightened up. When she looked again, the spider was gone.

The temperature in the room seemed to drop noticeably, and the light dimmed. Antonia shivered. She should have brought a sweater, as the day was cold and there was no insulation in the attic. But she knew the weather had nothing to do with the reason for her shivering.

She picked up her pad and pencil and left the attic without turning off the light.

"I can see that something has made an impression on you," Frederick said, coming into the kitchen where Antonia was sitting at the table with a twenty-ounce plastic bottle of soda. "You're looking for a quick caffeine fix."

"I needed it, all right," Antonia said. She took a drink from the bottle and set it on the table. "I have to ask you a few questions."

Frederick pulled out a chair and sat down across from her at the table.

"Something that you read?" he said.

"Yes," she said, and she told him about the sentence she had read in the book.

"That is interesting," Frederick said, obviously waiting for her response.

"Did you know I was going to find something like that?" she asked.

"If you mean, did I know you would find that exact sentence, the answer is no. I thought you might find something like it, however. And I did know that there has always been something...different about the women in this family, an unusual sensitivity to the psychic realm. Your sisters—well, you know your sisters. Do you remember what happened to Amanda when she opened the attic door?"

Antonia nodded. "I remember all too well. She warned me away from the attic, and I'm beginning to think I should have listened to her. I stayed away for years, but I didn't stay away long enough."

"Amanda was always the most sensitive, next to you," Frederick said.

Antonia had never thought of herself as being especially sensitive to anything, psychic or otherwise, except possibly to literature.

"What happened when Amanda opened that door?" Antonia asked.

"She never told me what she saw," Frederick said. "Nothing else happened, as far as I know."

"She never told me what she saw, either. Now I wish she had."

"Whatever it was, it does not matter now. At any rate, I expected that in your reading you might discover something similar to that sentence. You could be someone of unusual power. It just has to be tapped."

Antonia had another swallow of soda. Then she said, "I don't think my marriage to some thirteenth son is the way to go about it. This isn't the eighteenth century any longer, or haven't you noticed?"

"I am not quite that backward," Frederick said.

Antonia gave him a skeptical look, then smiled.

"Well, anyway there aren't any families that large these days. Nobody has a thirteenth son."

"I do not think the book was talking about just any family," Frederick said. "And you know better than to say there are no large families these days. There are the Derlichts."

Antonia got a hollow feeling in the pit of her stomach. She didn't like the way the conversation was going.

"I meant besides us," she said.

"Think about it for a minute," Frederick said. "I believe the last of the Noir boys was a few years ahead of you in high school, but you must have known about him."

"Martin," Antonia said. "Or Melvin. Something like that. He was six or seven years older than me. I don't remember him at all."

"His name is Mason," Frederick told her. "And he is the thirteenth son of James Noir."

Antonia tried to remember Mason Noir. Not much came back to her.

"He was pretty dorky in school," she said. "But he's probably married by now. Even a dork can find a wife these days if he half tries."

"He is not married," Frederick said.

Antonia fixed him with a suspicious glare.

"For somebody who claims not to have known about that particular sentence, you seem to know quite a lot about Mason Noir."

"Everyone in town knows about the Noirs. Those who are paying attention, at any rate. They are quite a prominent family."

"And one that you'd like to see take a fall," Antonia said. "You were hoping I'd find something to aid that cause, and now you think I have."

"I do not really know what you've found. It is true that I would love to see our own family take its rightful place among the great families of this state, and it is true that I believed the Noirs were the cause of our fall even before you started reading. But I had no idea what the route to our restoration might be."

Antonia finished off the soda and screwed the top back on the bottle. Frederick took it from her and dropped it into the recycle bin beside the refrigerator.

"I can tell you one thing," Antonia said. "I'm not marrying someone just because of some sentence written in a stupid old book in our attic."

She regretted having said it even before the words

were out of her mouth. Saying it was like admitting she knew the sentence had been addressed directly to her.

"No one is asking you to marry anyone," Frederick said. "But the book...well, you know that it has certain powers."

Antonia thought again about the way the runic scratchings had flowed into new shapes while she watched.

"I don't know *what* it has, but I still don't plan to marry anyone because of what it said. That would be ridiculous. You can't ask me to do it."

"I have already said I was not asking you. However..."

There was a silence that drew itself out for several seconds.

"Go on," Antonia said when she couldn't stand it any longer. "Finish your sentence. Were you going to say that the book might force me to marry? Is that it? Well, I don't believe it. That's even more ridiculous than my doing it on my own."

But when she thought of the way she'd felt in the attic, of the way the book had mysteriously allowed her to read it, of the feeling that the spider was watching her, she wasn't so sure just how ridiculous it was.

"I do not really know what powers there might be in a book or an old room," Frederick said. "Remember that the attic was build from the lumber that remained in the first Derlicht Haus, lumber that should by rights have been burned like the rest of the house, just as Agatha should have died."

"She was saved by Jonathan Noir, somehow or other."

"And how did he happen to be there? The attic of

Derlicht house is not the place where a member of the Noir family would be likely to visit."

"I don't know how he got there, and I don't see what difference it makes."

"Perhaps it makes none. Or perhaps we are talking about powers that are not as easy to ignore as you would like to think they are."

"I don't know why we're even talking about this," Antonia said. "I've never met Mason Noir, and he certainly doesn't know me. That would seem to be the end of it."

She should have felt relieved by that statement, but she didn't feel any different. If anything, she was more apprehensive than before.

"Do you have any mutual friends?" Frederick asked.

"I doubt it," Antonia said. "I haven't really talked with much of anyone since I started grad school. So unless Melvin is going to grad school at NYU ..."

"Mason," Frederick said. "Not Melvin."

"Whatever. I've never heard anyone mention him."

"There is a good reason for that. I believe he is something of an introvert, a rather solitary sort who prefers to keep to himself."

"So why would we have any mutual friends?"

"It was just a random thought. There must be some way that you can meet him."

Antonia sat up straight and put the palms of her hands flat on the tabletop.

"I don't plan to meet him. If he's some kind of hermit, he wouldn't be interested, anyway. Maybe he's gay.

Maybe he keeps his mummified mother in a rocking chair like Anthony Perkins in *Psycho*."

"I am surprised at you," Frederick said.

"Because I think Martin might be gay?"

"Not at all. I am surprised that you have seen *Psycho*. And his name is Mason. Why do you keep saying it incorrectly? Are you afraid to say it?"

Names have power, Antonia thought, without knowing where such a concept could have come from. And she had no idea why she resisted saying Mason's name. She knew very well what it was, yet something inside her resisted the pronunciation.

"It doesn't matter if I say it or not. I'm not interested in him, and he couldn't possibly be interested in me."

"You have not met him, so you cannot say for sure about the first. He has not met you, so you cannot know about the second."

She hated it that her father sounded so calm and reasonable. She didn't want to be reasonable. She wished she had never started her Special Project, or that she had chosen something, anything, else to work on.

"I think I need a little break from my work," she said. "Maybe I'll call someone and go to a movie tonight."

"You could call Mason Noir."

Her father said it with a straight face, and his tone betrayed no humor. Nevertheless, Antonia laughed.

"Now I know you're joking. You're so strait-laced that you'd never accept the idea that a woman could call a man and ask him out."

"I have changed with the times."

"No you haven't. Not in the least. You're just trying to provoke me."

"Well," Frederick said, and this time the corners of his lips did turn up a bit, "perhaps I am, but only a little."

"It won't work. I'm tired of being cooped up in a dusty old attic, and I'm going to a movie. But not with anybody like Mason Noir."

As soon as she said the name, a feeling of unease engulfed her. She gripped the edge of the table, hard, to keep her hand for trembling the way it had when she'd knocked the pencil off the table.

Frederick appeared not to notice anything out of the ordinary. He said, "Very well. Have it your way. But you may change your mind later on."

"Not a chance," Antonia said, hoping that she really meant it.

CHAPTER THIRTEEN

Mason sat on a stool in the workroom, staring at the wall but seeing nothing. The door to the workroom was locked and bolted from the inside. The door to the basement was also locked. But Mason did not feel secure.

He tried telling himself that he was acting like a child, which was true, but it was a lot more than that.

The man who had waved at him across the Mill Pond had looked like the one in the computer (*but there hadn't been anyone there!*), the one that Thomas Noir had attacked.

A ghost beside the Mill Pond in the middle of town, even with all the other people around, was somehow just as frightening as one inside a computer monitor, if not even more frightening. A ghost that was free to walk around in the open air could get to you anywhere.

Mason had always disregarded the stories of ghosts in Geiststadt. His father liked to tell about the ghosts all around them, the ones at HangedMan's Hill especially. Mason had considered them stories to scare kids with, nothing more but for once he was in danger of being convinced of the ghosts' existence.

What did the ghost want with him? That was obvious, since there was nothing other than MIND-NET that Mason owned or knew that anyone even a ghost would care about.

And if there were ghosts abroad, even locked doors wouldn't keep them out.

Mason got up from the stool and walked over to the workroom door. His hand hesitated for only a second, and then he unlocked the door.

Opening the door, he looked out into the basement. It had been finished and furnished as a game room when all the Noir boys were growing up. There was a table tennis set-up on one side of the room, and on the other there was an old Motorola television set. No one had turned it on for years as far as Mason knew. A dilapidated couch with a coffee table in front of it sat in about the middle of the room. There was nothing else there.

No ghost. Mason laughed at himself and went across the basement to unlock the other door. There was no ghost there either, and Mason went on upstairs and into the house. He heard his mother in the kitchen, and he went in to see what she had prepared for supper. He was glad to discover that he was hungry, and he was already beginning to dismiss his experience at the Mill Pond as another case of his over-stimulated imagination.

First, the stress had brought on the vision in the computer monitor.

Then that experience had prepared him to see something that wasn't there when he went on his walk. A case of the mind creating things it half-expected to see. It was all so obvious when he thought about it.

He was jumpier than a kangaroo, true. His nerves were unsettled as well. No doubt about that.

But he wasn't seeing ghosts. What an idiot he had been, locking himself in the workroom like that, as if he could keep an impalpable being out. He wouldn't be that foolish again, he assured himself.

The Noirs always ate the evening meal in the manor's huge dining room. Mason remembered that when he was a child there had been as many as sixteen people at the table at one time. Now there were only three, but Mason's parents insisted on keeping up the traditions. They could easily have afforded a cook, and they had kept one for years when all the brothers were there, but now that the family was so small, Laura Noir preferred to do the cooking herself.

Mason went by the dining room and into the kitchen. His mother was by the stove stirring a steaming pot, and his father sat in a chair at the small kitchen table reading a magazine.

James looked up when Mason walked in and laid the magazine on the table. Mason sat down across from him.

"Did you have a good walk?" James asked.

He had not seen Mason come rushing back to the house, and there was no insinuation in his voice. He didn't even bother to mention Mason's disheveled appearance.

"It was OK," Mason said.

He wasn't going to talk about what he thought he'd seen at the Mill Pond. There was no need to bring it up. It hadn't been real, after all.

"I'm sure it did you good," Laura said, not looking away from the stove. "I think it would be a good idea for you to get out more often."

Mason didn't think that would be a good idea at all. He didn't even want to go out for a haircut, not for a while. He said, "I might."

"You should go to a movie," his father said. "Maybe it would do you good."

Mason didn't think that would be a good idea, either. It wasn't that he was scared, he told himself. He just preferred to be at work on his experiments, that was all.

"I can watch a DVD if I want to see a movie," he said.

"There's nothing like the big screen," James said. "Better than a TV set or a computer monitor."

Again there was no insinuation, but Mason didn't like the mention of the computer monitor.

"You never know when you might meet someone interesting," James went on.

"I think I'll just stay here. At least for tonight. What's for dinner?"

"Spaghetti," Laura said. "One of your favorites."

"Great," Mason said.

Later that night, when Mason was in bed, he lay in his dark room and listened to the noises that filled the old house in the nighttime stillness: the sound of the wind in the eaves, the creaking noises that the wood made as the house seemed to shift itself to get more comfortable, the bumps on the roof when something fell from one of the big trees whose limbs overhung it, the rustling of the leaves, the rattling of a loose pane in one of the windows.

He remembered that when he was a child, he had shared this same room with three of his brothers, each of whom had a single bed of his own. The other beds had been moved out long ago, and Mason had filled the room with his own things, things he liked having around him: his favorite books, a couple of framed family photographs, a painting that he had done when he was taking an elective art class in college. On the rolltop desk there was an old Compaq computer, the first that Mason had ever owned. He couldn't see it because the top was rolled down, but he knew it was there. There was a CD player on a small table beside the desk, though Mason hadn't listened to much music lately. Nearby there was even an old exercise bike that Mason never rode.

With all those familiar things around him, Mason felt more secure and more certain that everything that had happened to him earlier that day had been tricks that his mind was playing on him because of the pressure he was under from his father.

Besides, Mason had put additional pressure on himself by leaving the house and walking around the town. He wasn't used to being out in the crowds of people, and he'd been nervous about it. His nervousness had contributed to his momentary panic.

The physical evidence that something had actually happened to him was more difficult to explain.

Yet even the comforting surroundings, even the sensible explanation for the bruise, didn't make Mason feel as much at ease as he would like to have felt.

For some reason, he found that he didn't want to go to sleep. He had never been much of a dreamer, or if he dreamed, he seldom remembered anything that he had dreamt. But tonight he dreaded the possibility of dreaming.

He didn't even want to close his eyes, as if the fact that he could no longer make out the dim shapes in the room might cause other shapes to appear there.

The thought that other shapes might appear even if he kept his eyes open didn't occur to him.

So, wide-eyed and sleepless, he listened to the noises of the house, and he thought about MIND-NET and all its possibilities. As exciting as those possibilities were, that thought led him to the worry of what might happen if James refused to give him any more money to continue his work. That would never do.

So Mason tried to imagine himself on a date with some attractive young woman, but it was impossible. He wouldn't even know how to ask for a date, something he hadn't done in years. And when he had asked girls out, years ago, he had been clumsy and embarrassed and half-glad that they turned him down more often than they accepted.

He tried to conjure up a portrait of the ideal woman, but nothing came to him. It was much easier to picture himself with someone a lot less than ideal, and, after all, it would be hard for him to find someone who shared his interests. Outside of books and computers, he didn't really have any.

Face it, Noir, he thought, *you have about as much chance of finding a woman who's compatible with you as a dog has of marrying a cat.*

If he was successful in what he was trying to do with MIND-NET, well, then things would be different. There were plenty of women who would want to know him then, and even if they didn't care about the accomplishment itself, much less understand it, they would be attracted to the prestige and the money that would come to him because of it. He wouldn't have to find them. They would seek him out.

But Mason didn't want a woman like that, and even if he did, the success of MIND-NET wasn't something that was going to come about overnight, or even over weeks or months. It would take years to see it to completion, and when those years had passed, it might turn out that his theories were all wrong. Even his father only half-believed in them. Sometimes Mason even doubted them himself.

But Thomas Noir doesn't doubt them, he thought. *Otherwise he wouldn't be trying so hard to get me to do what he wants, and warn me of what might happen to me if I don't do it his way.*

Mason was surprised to find that the thought of the ghost no longer frightened him as much. He stretched his arms and legs and began to relax.

As he did, a picture started to form in his mind. It was

almost as if he were seeing it on the ceiling of his darkened room, but of course that wasn't possible.

It was the figure of a woman.

The face wasn't quite clear to him, but he knew that it was very pretty. It was framed in long black hair (*of course it's black, you idiot; it's dark in here!*), and the eyes were blacker than the night outside. The woman was tall and slim, but not too slim, which was fine, because Mason's ideal woman wouldn't be skinny. Instead she would be almost regal looking. Like the one he was seeing there on the ceiling. There was intelligence in the wide-set eyes, and humor, too, which would be a necessary ingredient if a woman were going to date someone like Mason. There was also a sense of independence about her that pleased Mason. He didn't want a clingy woman who wouldn't understand his need for solitude and time alone with his experiments and his computer.

If he could only find that woman, he thought in complete disregard of thousands of years of human history, all his troubles would be over.

But of course he would never find her, because she existed only on the ceiling of his room and in the back of his mind.

Mason stared at the picture, but instead of disappearing it seemed to grow a bit clearer as the seconds passed. He shut his eyes, but when he opened them again the picture was still there. And it was getting clearer.

It was almost like the ghost, but a lot more pleasant, and Mason thought it was too bad that such a woman existed only in his head.

And then something happened that scared Mason even more than the ghost had.

The woman opened her mouth as if she were going to say something.

Mason tried to get his hands over his ears, but it was too late.

The woman spoke, and the word Mason heard was his name.

CHAPTER FOURTEEN

When Antonia awoke the next morning, the ragged edges of a dream flittered around in her head like the remnants of a shattered cloud.

She was irritated that all she could recall about the dream was that it had something to do with Mason Noir. She brushed her both her hair and her teeth too hard and suffered painful consequences. She hardly spoke to her father over breakfast, and when the telephone rang as she was about to go up to the attic, she answered it abruptly without checking the caller I.D.

The caller was a man who spoke poor English. He wanted to sell Antonia something, possibly a satellite dish, though she wasn't quite sure. She told him that she hated television and slammed the phone back into the cradle.

"You seem a bit touchy today," Frederick said. "I wonder why."

"It's nothing. I didn't sleep very well."

Frederick gave her a quizzical look. "Dreams?"

"No." Antonia paused. "All right, yes." She paused again. "Maybe."

"You should consider a career in politics," Frederick said. "You would be brilliant."

Antonia didn't feel like being jollied out of her bad mood, but she had to smile at her father's attempt at humor.

"I think I'll stick to being a student," she said. "And I won't drink so much soda today."

"I do not believe you can blame your dreams on caffeine."

Antonia didn't have to ask what he meant by that, but she did wonder if he knew more about her dreams than he was letting on.

"I have a suggestion," Frederick continued.

"About how to have a restful night's sleep? I don't need a suggestion. I usually sleep like a baby. Last night was an exception."

"It is not about your sleeping habits."

"Oh, all right. Let's have it."

"It is about Mason Noir," Frederick said.

"Oh. Then I'm not sure I want to hear it after all. I'm not the least bit interested in him."

"I think that is a mistake."

"Well, I don't." Antonia's black eyes snapped. "And if you think I'm going to marry him, you'd better think again."

"I wasn't talking about marriage. I was just wondering if the Noirs might not know more about their family history than you can find in those books. Or perhaps if they have similar records. If you could find another account of the past that tallies with the one you have already discovered, you could satisfy your committee about the authenticity. You might even find other information that you can use. It would certainly be worth talking to someone about."

It was something to think about, all right. What if the Noirs had records of their own family history that corroborated the story of Washington Irving's visit to Geiststadt and his role in the affair of the head-taker? That would be a big boost to Antonia's Special Project.

"You could call Mason," Frederick said. "You could tell him about your work and ask him to meet you to discuss it."

"Why don't I just call his parents?" Antonia said.

"They would likely be less receptive to the idea. There is still bad blood between our two families."

"Then why call at all?"

"Sometimes members of the younger generation do not have the same animosities that their parents possess," Frederick said. "You have read *Romeo and Juliet*, I know."

Antonia had read it, of course, but she didn't like the implications.

"I did not mean that you would fall madly in love with Mason Noir and die in a tomb," Frederick told her when he saw the look on her face. "I meant that young people do not hold the grudges of their parents."

"You're holding it," Antonia pointed out. "Just as your own parents must have done."

"Ah, but that is different. My generation was different from yours in many ways, just as my parents' generation was different from my own. My father would regard me as having been very lax in my duties for not having passed along our enmity for the Noirs. I tried with some of your older sisters, Amelia and Andrea especially, but they would have none of it."

Frederick sighed and stared off into space with unfocused eyes. Whether he was seeing the faces of her sisters or that of his own disapproving father, Antonia did not know.

"At any rate," Frederick said after a few seconds, snapping back to the present, "you are not infected with my own antipathy to the Noir family. You could call Mason and see what he has to say. It would cost you nothing."

Antonia wanted to ask why he was so insistent on her making the call if his antipathy was genuine, but she knew the answer. If there was a chance of returning some power to the Derlichts, Frederick was in favor of it. A phone call was nothing to him. Even a marriage would be acceptable.

Antonia put the thought of marriage out of her mind, but she couldn't avoid the thought that her father might be right. The Noirs might very well have information that she could use, and, as Frederick said, it would cost her nothing to find out.

"All right," she said. "I'll call."

Fredrick's smug look vanished almost as soon as it appeared, but Antonia saw it. She chose, however, to ignore it.

"I'll call later," she said. "I want to read the newspaper first."

"As you choose," Frederick said, but when he left the room, he was smiling.

Mason answered the phone because no one else would. He knew why when he saw the Derlicht name on the caller I.D. However, as far as he was concerned, there was no reason not to answer it and at least one good reason to do so. No Derlicht had ever called there that he could remember, and if one of them was doing so, there might be some kind of emergency.

"Hello," he said.

"Is this the Noir residence?"

The voice sounded strangely familiar to Mason, but that was impossible of course, and he dismissed the idea at once.

"Yes, this is Mason Noir. Who's calling?"

"My name is Antonia Derlicht. We went to school together. Do you remember me?"

Mason's school years had not been happy ones. He had been too much of a nerd to run with the popular crowd, even if he was from a family that the community held in high esteem. He had kept to himself and had never really mingled with his classmates.

"Not really," he said. "Were you in my class?"

"No. I was a few years behind you."

"Oh," Mason said.

It was all he could think of, even though he liked the voice and would have liked to continue the conversation my making some suitably clever remark. He might come up with something later, say two or three days later, but it was typical that when he needed his wits most, they were somewhere else.

"Maybe you remember my sisters," Antonia said. "Amanda was in your class, I believe."

Mason remembered Amanda, but only vaguely. She was an attractive girl, but she never said much and looked a little frightened all the time.

"I remember her," Mason said, wondering if Antonia was getting together a high school reunion or something similar. Mason had never been to one of those, and he planned never to attend one. He started getting his excuses ready. "Why?"

"No reason," Antonia told him. "I was wondering if we had any mutual friends. You see, there's something I'd like to discuss with you, and I thought it might be easier if we could establish some connections."

"You'd like to discuss something with me?" Mason asked.

He could never remember a woman wanting to discuss anything with him, and he couldn't imagine why this one would want to. She was a Derlicht, after all.

"Yes. About our families and their histories. It's for a paper I'm writing at NYU."

"A paper?"

"For my Special Project. It's about urban legends."

Mason didn't get it. What did urban legends have to do with his family or the Derlichts?

Antonia seemed to sense his puzzlement. She said, "This would be a lot easier if we could meet in person. I could explain things more clearly."

Mason looked over his shoulder. Neither of his parents was in sight. He said, "That sounds OK."

The thought of suggesting a time or a place for a meeting never entered his head. Antonia was beginning to wonder if he was a little slow on the uptake.

"Do you know Fauntleroy's?" she asked.

Mason had passed the place the day before, but he'd never been inside. It was a trendy updating of an old-time ice-cream parlor.

"I know where it is," he said.

"Good. I could meet you there this morning if that would be all right. I'll explain what I'm doing and why you might be able to help me."

"This morning?"

Antonia suppressed a sigh. "Yes. Around ten o'clock. Would that be all right?"

Mason looked at his wristwatch: 9:30.

"That sounds all right."

"Good. I'll see you there, then?"

"I'll be there," Mason said.

After he hung up the phone, Mason started to think about the implications of the call. It all seemed a little too pat to him. Almost as soon as his father had become insistent that Mason get out of the house and meet someone, a woman calls and wants to talk to him. But his father couldn't have arranged it. Not with a Derlicht.

Mason looked around again to be sure he was alone. His parents would never approve of him seeing Antonia Derlicht, much less marrying her. The Derlicht family and the Noirs were not even on speaking terms. Mason wasn't quite sure why, but he knew it was the case.

No matter what his parents might think, however, he sincerely wanted to meet Antonia. There was something about her voice that appealed to him, and if she looked anything like her sister, she was no doubt quite attractive.

But seeing her would mean leaving the house again. Mason wasn't sure he wanted to do that, not after yesterday's little episode.

On the other hand, what had happened? Nothing. The "ghost" hadn't been real, and neither had anything else. No harm was going to come to him if he met a woman for a malt. It would be like a date in an episode of some old 1950s TV show like the ones on Nickelodeon, *Leave it to Beaver* or another one like that.

As for his parents and any objections that they might have, that was easy. Mason just wouldn't tell them what he was going to do. After all, his mother had said it would do him good to get out more often.

So Mason got his jacket and went to tell his mother that he was going for another walk, his second in as many days. He was becoming a real adventurer. Except that he hoped he wouldn't be having any adventures. He wanted a nice, quiet walk with no ghostly appearances, thank you very much. Not that he was expecting any. His stress level had dropped quite a bit since the previous evening, maybe because he had gotten a good night's sleep. He hadn't expected to, but he had drifted off while listening to the noises of the night, and the next thing he knew it was morning.

He remembered nothing of the figure that he had seen on the ceiling, and even had he done so, he would have dismissed it as a figment of his reverie-prone mind. He would have seen it as just another example of how his father's pressure to find a wife had affected him.

He stepped out onto the porch of the house. It was a beautiful day. Though it was still cold, the sun was shining, and the sky was a clear cerulean blue.

Mason walked down the steps and onto the walk. After he had gone a few yards, he turned and looked back at the house. The rays of the sun struck the *uraeus* symbol that was set above the main entrance to Noir Manor. The *uraeus* was made of gold leaf, blue and red enamel, and jet inlay. A kind of Noir family crest, it consisted of a winged sun disk with a snake that might have been a cobra writhing under it.

Mason wasn't fond of snakes, but the emblem was so familiar to him that he didn't think of it as being frightening. It reminded him of home, and it had always been comforting for him to see it.

Now, however, it appeared more sinister, though Mason could not have said why. He shivered in the sun, and he looked around to see if anyone might be watching him.

No one was, but that knowledge did not make Mason any more comfortable. He felt an itch between his shoulder blades, as if someone's eyes were focused there.

I'm being stupid again, he told himself. *Or maybe I'm nervous because I'm going to meet a woman I don't know and have never even seen before.*

Mason turned back to the walk, and his step quickened as he moved away from Noir Manor.

He wondered what Antonia Derlicht looked like.

He wondered if she would like him. He didn't think

there was much chance of that unless his luck with wo-men had changed drastically over the last few years. And he had no reason to believe that it had.

Nevertheless, it promised to be an interesting meeting, and Mason was suddenly eager for it to take place. He hardly noticed anyone else on the street, and by the time he got to the end of the block, he was almost running.

CHAPTER FIFTEEN

Fauntleroy's was sandwiched between a Starbuck's and a Half-Price Books. It had twenty-seven flavors of ice cream, and for those whose tastes ran to more than plain ice cream there were shakes, sundaes, splits, floats and malts. Customers who wanted something resembling an actual meal could chose from ten varieties of hamburgers with fries or onion rings. And there were also fresh-baked cookies.

The tables were small and round with granite tops, and the chairs were made of wrought iron. There was a working soda fountain, and the young men behind it were dressed like soda jerks from an earlier time. There was a jukebox stocked with music that had been recorded no later than the 1960s. Something by Elvis Presley was playing when Antonia walked inside.

It was all a little precious for her tastes, but she liked the way the smell of the cooking hamburgers mingled with the smell of baking cookies. She hadn't chosen the place because of its smell, however. She had chosen it because it was easy to find, there were plenty of people around, and it was noisy enough so that nobody was going to overhear anything she said to Mason Noir.

She sat at a table and watched the door. She had looked at Mason's picture in an old high school yearbook to refresh her memory. He hadn't looked quite as dorky as she'd thought, and she hoped she'd know him when she saw him.

When he walked through the door, she recognized him at once. His hair was a little too long, but aside from that he was quite presentable, and much better-looking than she had expected. Getting older had definitely helped him.

Maybe this wouldn't be so bad after all, Antonia told herself as she raised a hand to wave at him.

Mason stood just inside the door of the ice-cream parlor and looked around. When he saw the woman waving at him, he felt as if someone had slugged him in the heart with a rubber hammer. She was beautiful, and although he knew he'd never seen her before, she looked instantly familiar. Maybe he had met her in school, though he certainly didn't remember it, and he was almost certain he would remember anyone who looked the way she did. People change, though, so she might look much different now from the girl she had been in those days.

He started toward the place where she was sitting and stubbed his toe on a table leg. A man sitting at the table dropped his spoon, which clanked off the hard tabletop and fell to the floor. Mumbling apologies, Mason bent to pick up the spoon and bumped heads with the man who had dropped it. Startled, Mason straightened up quickly. He took a step backward and collided with a woman who was carrying a bowl of ice cream in one hand and a float in the other. She stumbled awkwardly, juggling the bowl and glass, and came to a stop against another table, rattling everything on it. A woman sitting there grabbed her and saved her from falling.

Mason's face flamed, and he apologized again to everyone around him. Finally he got away and made it safely to Antonia's table.

"That was quite an entrance," she said. "You must be Mason Noir."

"That's me." Mason tried to make a joke of what had happened. "Or you can call me Grace Personified."

"I'll stick with Mason. Do you want any ice cream?"

Mason thought they'd better order something if they were going to sit there and talk. "Sure, that sounds good. Thanks."

"What would you like?"

"Just a dip of vanilla."

"Sit down, then. I'll be right back."

As Antonia went to get the ice cream, the jukebox was playing something about "at the hop" by a group Mason had never heard before. He thought she knew what a hop was, however, and figured that when it came to dancing, he'd be better off on the sidelines. He'd almost destroyed Fauntleroy's just trying to walk from the door to her table.

Mason sat at the small table and watched her walk to the counter to place the order. She was as graceful as he was clumsy, he thought, with long legs and a dancer's walk. He might as well leave right now. He was never going to get anywhere with a woman who looked like that.

It wasn't long before Antonia came back with two small bowls of vanilla ice cream and set them on the table. She smiled at Mason and sat down across from him.

"Thanks," Mason said, pulling the bowl of ice cream toward himself and taking a napkin from a black metal and chrome holder in the middle of the table. There was a glass full of plastic spoons beside the napkin holder, so he took one of those as well.

"I know you must be curious about my Special Project," Antonia said, settling into her chair.

Mason had no real idea what a Special Project was, but he didn't want to say so. He told Antonia that he was indeed curious.

"It's a paper I have to write to get my master's degree," Antonia told him. "I'm a student at NYU, and it's one of the requirements."

Mason remembered that she had mentioned that on the phone. He said, "You're writing about urban legends?"

"That's right," Antonia said, pleased that he'd remembered. "We have quite a few of them right here in Geiststadt. I'm sure you know some of them."

Mason didn't know them, but he didn't want to display his ignorance. So he said, "Right," and ate a bite of ice cream.

"There's the one about the head-taker," Antonia said. "That's probably the most famous one."

Mason was on firmer ground there. He'd heard that story ever since he'd been a child.

"Yes. I know that one. My brothers used to scare me with it when we were growing up. I never believed it, of course."

"Well, you should." Antonia took another bite of ice cream. "It's true."

Mason was surprised. He didn't think anybody thought there was anything to those old stories.

"Really?" he said. "I thought it was just something people told their kids to keep them quiet or that my big brothers used to scare me."

"Oh, no. There really was a series of beheadings right here in the early nineteenth century." Antonia had decided not to mention how directly involved Mason's family had been, at least not yet. "That's what my paper is about."

"About the beheadings?"

"No. Well, not entirely. That story will be just a part of it, but only a part. I'm looking into the sources of the legends, to see if they're based on actual events. And in this case, the answer is yes."

"You have proof?"

"Sort of," Antonia said. Mason sounded as if he were one of her committee members. "That's one of the things I wanted to talk to you about."

Mason shook his head and grinned ruefully.

"You came to the wrong guy, then," he said. "I don't know anything about it. And I don't think much of 'sort of' proof. I'm a scientist. I like things that I can verify."

Antonia decided to change her approach slightly and

let Mason talk about himself. Men liked to do that, or so everyone told her.

"What kind of scientist are you?" she asked.

Mason didn't want to go into MIND-NET with a stranger, not even to impress one as beautiful as this. He said, "I work with computers."

"That's interesting. I took some computer courses as an undergrad. Not that I'm a whiz or anything. What's your specialty?"

Mason ate some ice cream to avoid answering. After a few seconds he said, "I'm working on several things. Nothing that would mean much to you, though."

Antonia wondered if she should be insulted but decided to let it go. The conversation wasn't working out as well as she'd hoped. Might as well get to the crux of the matter.

"Did you ever think about the similarity of the stories of the head-taker to Washington Irving's story about the Headless Horseman?"

Antonia didn't really think Mason would have read the story, but she hoped he might have seen some cartoon version or at least have heard of it.

To her surprise he said, "Yes, I've read the story. I like Irving. I've read the whole *Sketch Book*."

"You have?"

"Sure. You don't think a computer guy can like to read?"

That was pretty much Antonia's conception, or misconception. To smooth things over she said, "I just pictured you as more of a reader of nonfiction."

"I keep up in my field, but we Noirs are great readers

of fiction. You should see our library. We have all kinds of first editions of modern authors, and a lot of the older ones, too. I learned to read before I ever went to school, and I've been reading ever since."

Antonia was pleased to discover that she and Mason had something in common. She told him about her own reading, Mason described the family library, and they discovered that they liked many of the same writers. They even shared an interest in Poe and Irving.

"I don't believe any of that supernatural stuff, though," Mason said. "it makes for a good story, but in real life I'm interested in rational explanations for everything."

"There's a rational explanation for the beheadings that happened here," Antonia told him, looking down that ice cream that had mostly melted in the bowl in front of her. "I should think you'd know about that."

"Why should I?"

Instead of answering, Antonia asked about the books in the library he'd been telling her about.

"Do you have any old family journals? And records from the time of Benjamin Noir?"

Mason's head jerked up. He didn't like the direction the conversation was taking.

"No. We don't have anything like that at all."

Antonia wondered about his reaction. "Then how do you keep up with the family history?"

"We don't, and I for one don't want to. There's nothing in that past that interests me. I care about the future, not what happened a hundred years ago."

"But what about your ancestors? Don't you want to know your heritage?"

Mason started to sweat, and his eyes got wild.

"No! There's nothing in the past that I care about, especially not my ancestors. Let the dead stay dead."

He stood up, threw his napkin on the table and turned to go. Antonia thought about trying to stop him, but before she could say anything, he had bumped into a woman carrying a small child. The three of them did an awkward dance around a couple of tables before getting themselves stabilized. Mason apologized to the woman and managed to get out the door without further embarrassing himself.

Antonia watched him go, wondering why she had even bothered with him. He was an uncoordinated oaf, and he didn't want to talk about his family, or at least his forerunners. He claimed that he didn't know anything about them, but she could tell that he was lying. He wouldn't have acted so rudely if he had been completely ignorant of them.

That made her curious. What did he know, and why wouldn't he talk about it?

Maybe he did know about the head-taker and the story of Thomas and Jonathan Noir. If he did, she'd like to hear his version of it. But not enough to beg him. She didn't beg. If he didn't want to talk, she could find confirmation of the information in the old journal elsewhere. Or not.

Her father would be disappointed when she told him about the meeting. She certainly wouldn't be marrying a thirteenth son if Mason Noir was the only one available. She had no interest in him at all.

Another Elvis Presley song came on the jukebox, something about a teddy bear.

Antonia decided it was time she got out of there.

Mason felt like a fool. He didn't know why he'd reacted as he had, except that the mention of Benjamin Noir had reminded him of Thomas, and that was one ancestor whose existence Mason wanted very much to forget.

But forgetting wasn't easy, and the memory all the things that had happened (*not really; they were only imagination!*) came flooding back into Mason's head. He ducked into the bookstore next door to Fauntleroy's. His breathing was quick and shallow, and his heart was pounding. He hid himself in the aisles to recover and to get himself under control.

Standing there, he thought he saw someone familiar walk by the window in front of the store.

It was himself.

Or someone who looked a lot like him.

Thomas Noir, Mason thought, not wanting to think it but unable not to.

He's looking for me, Mason thought.

He looked around the store and located a back door leading to an alley. He went out that way and hurried home even faster than he had moved in getting to Fauntleroy's for the meeting.

CHAPTER SIXTEEN

I'm sorry," the man said, as if it were his fault that Antonia almost walked into him outside of Starbuck's.

And it was his fault in a way, Antonia thought. She hadn't been watching where she was going, but he seemed to have appeared out of nowhere. He looked like someone she should have known, but she didn't know who it might have been.

"It was my fault," Antonia said, being gracious.

"No, no. I was careless. Please accept my apology."

He spoke with an odd accent, as if he might have learned English as a foreign language.

"It's quite all right," Antonia said. "I was in a hurry and didn't see you."

The man nodded and walked away. Antonia watched him go, and he faded from sight.

Literally. He was moving along the walk with the other pedestrians when all at once his shape wavered like heat rising from a desert. Then he was gone, as if he had never been there at all.

Antonia put up a hand to shade her eyes from the

glare of the sun, but no sign of him remained. Her life was getting stranger by the day. First the book and the spider and now strangers that seem familiar and then disappear in broad daylight.

"I want to know about Thomas Noir," Mason said.

He and James were in the library. Laura was elsewhere in the house, and Mason had taken the opportunity to speak to his father alone.

"What would you like to know?" James asked.

He sat in the chair by the window, where he had been reading a novel by Philip Roth.

"Whatever you can tell me."

"You've seen him again?"

"No," Mason said. "Yes. Maybe. I don't know."

"I'd say that covers just about every possibility. You don't seem pleased about it."

"I've heard a...rumor."

"What might that be?"

"That the head-taker stories are based on something that really happened, and that our family was involved."

Mason knew what he was saying wasn't quite true. Antonia had implied a connection between the Noirs and the beheadings, but she hadn't said there was one. Still, it seemed highly likely to Mason that she had been about to.

James laid his book aside and said, "I don't know anything about that, not really. Our family has never been one to flaunt the dirty laundry. If there's some truth to those stories, it's possible Benjamin or Thomas could have had something to do with them. They weren't as civilized as we are. They would have stopped at nothing to achieve their goals."

Mason noted the curl of James's lip when he pronounced the word *civilized*. And he thought he detected approval of the ambitions of his ancestors. After all, those ambitions weren't so different from James's, Mason thought. But James was indeed more civilized, whether he was proud of that fact or not.

"Don't we have any old records set down by the family? Any old family histories that I could read?"

"No," James said. "But you've met Thomas. I should think that would be enough for you."

"I haven't met anybody. That was a hallucination brought on by stress, that's all."

"You can think what you like," James said. He picked up his book and turned to his place.

Mason left the room and went down to the basement, where he sat on the old couch and brooded. He had acted like a clown at his meeting with Antonia, nearly wrecking the restaurant like one of the Three Stooges. Or all of them. Then he had run out on her before finding out what she had really wanted to tell him, all because she had reminded him of some unpleasant imagined experiences. She had put the idea of Thomas in his mind again, and that explained why he thought he'd seen him outside the bookstore. He felt silly about that now.

But it didn't explain something else. Mason sat up straight on the couch as he realized what it was. He hadn't been to the study since the day before. He always spent a lot of time there with his computer, working out calculations for MIND-NET, but today he hadn't gone there. He had run to the basement, a place where he rarely went except to pass through it on his way to the workroom.

He shook his head in derision and told himself that he wasn't avoiding the study, not at all. He'd had to go to meet Antonia, and he hadn't had time for the study. He had time now, though. He'd just go right on up there and see if everything was all right.

But even as he told himself what he would do, he sank back into the cushions of the couch. He wasn't going anywhere, not just yet.

Another thing that bothered him was that he found Antonia very attractive. It wasn't just her beauty, though he had to admit that was a big part of it. But added to beauty was intelligence. They hadn't talked long, but he had heard enough to know that she was well read and had thought about what she had read. She hadn't just looked at the words. She had absorbed them and their meaning.

In short, she was just the kind of woman he'd always hoped to find someday, and now that he had, he'd blown his chances by acting like a crazy man.

He was sure his father wouldn't approve of his dating a Derlicht, no matter how desperate James was for Mason to start a family of his own, but if Mason ever did marry, Antonia Derlicht would be perfect as far as he was concerned. He wished he hadn't acted like such an idiot at Fauntleroy's, but there was nothing he could do about that now.

But that was a stupid way to think. All he had to do

was pick up the phone and call her. He could apologize for the way he'd acted and ask if he could see her again.

If he did, however, she would want to talk about Thomas Noir again, and Mason didn't like that at all. Just thinking about it made him start sweating again.

Why? Mason wondered.

It shouldn't affect him that way. He was a scientist, a rational man, and he shouldn't be troubled in the least by the idea of discussing a man who had been dead for well over a hundred years.

It was all the extraordinary things that had been happening lately, he decided. (*Not that they had actually happened!*) They were warping his judgement, making him act in ways that weren't really reflective of his personality. OK, he had to admit that he was clumsy. Wrecking the ice cream shop wasn't out of character at all, though he was nervous because he was going to meet Antonia.

Would he be equally nervous if he went to meet her again? Yes, but it would be worth it. And if she tried to discuss Thomas, Mason could change the subject.

There was a phone in the basement. It sat on a thick directory on top of the TV set, and Mason looked over at it. He didn't know Antonia's number, but he could easily find it in the directory. Unless the Derlichts were unlisted, and Mason didn't think that was the case.

Call her, you dope, he thought.

He had started to get up and go for the phone when the TV set clicked on.

At first Mason thought he must have somehow touched the remote, but then he saw it on the coffee table.

He looked back at the TV set. There was no picture yet, just a bright blue spot in the middle of the screen. The dot was slowly growing larger.

Oh, no, Mason thought, remembering his experience with the computer monitor in the study and the lab. *Not again.*

He got up to run from the room, but the pull of the TV was too strong for him to resist. This time he was being drawn in feet first, and he managed to grab the coffee table with both hands. It was short and squat, made of good maple hardwood. He gripped it as if it were a life preserver as he was drawn across the room. It didn't slow him down in the least, but he didn't let it go.

This isn't happening. The words repeated over and over in his head, but it was hard to deny the evidence of his senses.

His feet disappeared inside the set, meeting no resistance. It was as if the glass front had dissolved.

"No!" Mason yelled, determined that he wasn't going to meet Thomas Noir again, either in reality or in his imagination, whichever was responsible for what was going on. "I'm not going!"

He clung to the coffee table, and as he was sucked completely into the old Motorola, he felt the table hit the edges of the screen. He hoped that whatever was affecting him would not be able to affect the table. It didn't. His progress stopped. There was still the feeling of a powerful suction, and he thought that his clothes might be pulled off, but he wasn't going anywhere.

He began to struggle against the force that was trying to overwhelm him, trying to inch himself past the coffee table. It didn't seem that it would be possible, but then getting pulled into a TV set wasn't possible, either. But it had happened.

Or perhaps he was only imagining it. Well, if he could imagine that, he could imagine saving himself.

His muscles strained to their utmost, and veins popped up on his forearms. He felt his shoes fly off, and that gave him a burst of adrenaline that allowed him to force his head past the side of the coffee table and back into the basement room. As soon as he did that, he felt the suction lessen, and he kicked like an Olympic swimmer while pulling at the same time.

There was a *pop* as he flew out of the TV set and landed on the floor. The coffee table landed right on top of him, and Mason lay there for a few seconds as he tried to orient himself.

He raised his head to see if the TV set was still on. The glass front reflected the light of the room, but there was only darkness behind it.

Mason shoved the coffee table aside and got up. Looking down at his feet, he saw that he wasn't wearing any shoes.

He turned to the TV set again. It just couldn't be that his shoes were somewhere inside it. And they weren't. They were lying right in front of it. Either the Motorola had belched them out, or they had been there all along.

Mason started to explain things to himself in the way he usually did. He had taken his shoes off to get more comfortable and fallen asleep on the couch, where he'd dreamed that he was being pulled into the TV set. The dream had become a nightmare, and he had rolled off the couch, grabbing the coffee table as he fell. He had turned over and dragged the table on top of him, and then he had awakened.

There it was, a perfectly logical explanation for everything that had happened.

But it occurred to Mason that he was spending an awful lot of time lately in thinking up explanations. And even though they made sense, they weren't as satisfactory as he'd like for them to be, not any longer. What if something really were happening to him. What if his father was right and strange forces were stirring in Geiststadt? Where did Mason fit in? Maybe Antonia could give him some answers.

He shook his head and decided that he would go to his room. He didn't want to stay in the basement any longer.

CHAPTER SEVENTEEN

Antonia sat in her attic and pored over the old book as if it contained the secrets of the universe instead of just the secrets of the Derlichts and the Noirs. There was a new intensity to her studies, and she attributed it to two things.

One was her encounter at Fauntleroy's. Not her rendezvous with Mason, but her brief meeting with the other man. She wouldn't call herself a believer in the paranormal, but her experiences over the last couple of days had convinced her that *something* unusual was going on in her world. Was the man she'd seen an apparition, perhaps the ghost of one of the Noirs, and that he had been watching her and Mason?

The second was her feeling that there was some kind of presence in the attic. She had felt it before, but never so acutely as now. It was almost as if someone were peering over her shoulder.

There was a noise behind her, and she looked away from the journal. A spider bustled along the wainscot. It stopped and stared back at her. She felt suddenly light-headed, and the air in the attic turned stuffy and suffoc-

ating seconds before a chill wind penetrated the room
with a biting cold.

Antonia stood up, pushing back the chair, but she sat
back down at once. The room spun before her eyes, and
dizziness came over her. She tried to stand again, bracing
her hands on the table where the book sat. She managed
not to fall to the floor, falling instead across the table
just before she lost consciousness.

When she awoke, Antonia raised her head and looked
around the attic. Nothing had changed, and she wondered
how long her dizzy spell had lasted. Not long, she
thought, though she felt refreshed, as if she had slept for
hours.

Her eyes returned to the table, and she jumped back
as if she had been bitten by a snake. Or a spider.

What had frightened her was nothing much, just a
book lying there.

But it was a book that had not been there before. It
lay beside the old journal, but Antonia knew that she
had not put it there.

It was small, like a diary, and it too was bound in
leather. Antonia was certain that it had not been on the
shelves in the attic. She had looked at all the books rather
carefully. This one had not been among them.

Her head was clear now. No trace of dizziness remained. She reached out a hand to touch the book, and
the cover flipped open of its own accord. Antonia's invisible assistant was helping out again. Perhaps that had
been the presence she felt.

The first page of the book contained only a few words,

but they were words that gave Antonia a chill: "Agatha Derlicht. Her Diary."

Antonia had a feeling that she now knew who her assistant was. Agatha had nearly met her death in the old attic, the one from whose boards this one was made. Something of her spirit remained here, Antonia was certain. She pulled the chair to the table, sat in it, and began to read.

When she put the book aside at last, Antonia leaned back in the chair and sighed. If Agatha was to be believed, and Antonia saw no reason not to believe, the Derlicht family was gifted with powers far beyond those of ordinary folk. Antonia had seen enough evidence of that to convince her that it was true in what had happened with the books.

But Agatha went on to write that the Noirs were also gifted. However, the Noirs, unlike the Derlichts, were intent on gaining even more power, and in doing so they often caused suffering to others. Sometimes they even chose to inflict the suffering.

A case in point was Thomas Noir, who was not only behind the gruesome murders in his own time, but who, as Antonia had learned from her reading, tried to destroy Agatha and all the Derlicht family into the bargain. In some way, though (and Agatha did not make this clear in the diary), Jonathan Noir had saved her from the great fire that Thomas had caused to consume Derlicht Haus.

As a result of the fire, Agatha developed an almost pathological hatred of the Noir family, and it came through powerfully in the pages she had written. Her pen might have been dipped in hatred. Even the fact that a Noir had saved her did not change her mind. As she said, he would not have had to save her had his brother not tried to kill her.

Jonathan had lost his own life in the fire, dying to prevent Agatha's death, but that meant nothing to her except that Jonathan "must not have been a true Noir, but rather some kind of imposter, nurtured from the womb to foil his brother's evil designs."

Reading these things, Antonia knew that she had to see Mason Noir again. She had to find out his side of the story and see if he knew of the psychic powers that Agatha attributed to his family.

She had no idea how to go about talking to Mason again, but she knew she would think of something, and quickly. She couldn't pass up this opportunity. For here was the origin of another urban legend.

The old tales around Geiststadt had it that Derlicht Haus had been destroyed by a great storm, one of preternatural power and intensity.

There may well have been a storm, but the fire that had kindled Derlicht Haus had come not from lightning but from Thomas Noir.

Or perhaps he had created the lightning. At any rate, she had to learn more, and she was convinced that Mason could help her.

Then something else dawned on her. She had only that day encountered one of the most prominent urban legends, and she hadn't even given it any thought.

All her life she had heard stories of the ghosts of Geiststadt, but she had never seen one. Until today, that is. And when she had, it had not even struck her as unusual.

And she was sure it was the ghost of Jonathan Noir. There were stories that Jonathan appeared in Geiststadt in times of trouble, but Antonia had simply added them to her list of urban legends. However, it seemed that there was a factual basis for them, and that Jonathan had returned.

Why today? Were her own latent psychic powers becoming more developed by her contact with these ghosts? Her heart pounded at the exciting possibility. Or could there have been some other reason?

Whatever the reason, she knew that the old stories were true, and Geiststadt was indeed haunted, by one ghost at least. And if there was one, there could be more.

She wondered if Mason Noir had seen any ghosts. Now there was another reason for her to get in touch with him and get to know him better.

As she sat there thinking about a way to approach him, there was a knock on the attic door.

"It's open," she said, and Frederick came into the room.

"I'm sorry to disturb you," he said. "But you have a phone call. I thought it might be important."

"Who is it?" Antonia said, wondering if it was from someone at NYU. She hoped nothing had happened to Dr. Martin.

"A young man," Frederick said. "He told me that his name was Mason Noir."

Antonia took the call, of course.

Mason was apologetic for having bothered her. He

said that knew her studies were important, but he wanted to apologize for his behavior and for embarrassing himself and her in Fauntleroy's.

"You didn't embarrass me at all," Antonia assured him, in full charm mode.

She was pleased that he had called her, saving her the trouble of having to invent some excuse to meet him again, and she wasn't going to let him get away so easily this time.

"I know you're curious about my family's history," Mason said, "and I thought we could talk some more about that."

He hadn't been eager to talk earlier, Antonia thought, and she wondered what had changed his mind. She didn't ask, however. She would find out later.

"I'd love to talk to you again," she said, putting just the slightest emphasis on *love*. "When can we meet?"

"Uh, well, I hadn't thought about that," Mason said. "I wasn't sure you'd even take my call."

"Of course I'd take your call. I'll tell you what. Why don't you come over here tonight? I'm very interested in what you have to tell me."

Mason didn't know what to say to that. He didn't plan to tell her anything if he could avoid it. He just wanted to see her again. And meet her at Derlicht Haus? He didn't think a Noir had been to Derlicht Haus in well over a century. The families just didn't get along.

"Are you sure it would be all right?" he said. "For me to come over there, I mean."

"I don't see why not. You can come after dinner. We can have dessert and coffee."

"Well, I guess I could do that."

"Good. I'll be expecting you about eight o'clock. Would that be all right?"

Mason said it would be fine and hung up. Now the question was, should he tell his parents what he was going to do?

He was, after all, over thirty years old, and he could do what he pleased, even visit a Derlicht. He didn't even have to tell his parents if he didn't feel like it.

They would be very suspicious, however, if he left the house at night, considering his predilection for staying inside. Even though he had left twice within the last two days, neither time had been at night.

He would have to wait and see what they said when he told them. He would either tell them the truth or lie, whichever seemed best at the time.

With that unhappy thought, Mason went up to his room. He should have gone to the study, or to the workroom to check on his computers, but he didn't want to see either the computer monitor in the study or the TV screen in the basement. Not until he was feeling a little better about things.

He wasn't really avoiding them, just being prudent, and he was determined that his meeting with Antonia would put him in a better frame of mind. How could it not? She was the woman he had always wanted.

CHAPTER EIGHTEEN

A place outside of space and time is not really a place at all.

Nevertheless it existed, and two spirits met there.

"You are trying to interfere," Thomas Noir said. "I will not abide that."

"You will," Jonathan told him, "for there is nothing you can do about it."

"It was enough that you sent Mason back when I had him the first time. You have given him strength, and he was able to resist me later. I will not tolerate any more."

"You will," Jonathan repeated. "You work your work, and I work mine."

"As it ever was, my brother."

"Yes," Jonathan said, "as it ever was."

"This time the end will be different."

"We shall see."

"This time, I shall have what I seek. I will once again walk the world of men and taste its pleasures. This time I will not lose."

"You walk the world now."

"But not as a man walks. Only as a spirit, and a spirit does not taste the joys of life. You deprived me of those once, but I will have them again. I will do what I wished to do so long ago, and Mason will be my gateway."

"No," Jonathan said. "He will not."

"He will. This time the Derlichts will pay, and you will not prevent me."

"You never lacked confidence, Thomas. It is too bad that you lacked a moral sense."

"One does not miss what one does not need, my brother."

The two spirits parted again, if indeed they had ever been together in a place that could not exist, but did.

CHAPTER NINETEEN

Mason's driving was much worse than his walking. He hadn't driven in several years, so the darkness of the cloudy night and the glare of the lights both served to confuse and disorient him. There were a couple of times when he wondered if he would arrive at Derlicht Haus without being involved in an accident. He knew there would be several other drivers who would remember him for quite a while and who would be thankful that he had managed to miss them completely when it appeared that he would smash right into them.

Ordinarily, he would have walked to Derlicht Haus just to avoid having to get behind the wheel. The excuse he gave his father for taking the car was that it was too cold to walk, but the real reason was that Mason didn't want to chance running into someone who looked like Thomas Noir on a dark street at night.

Derlicht Haus was on the north side of Geiststadt, not far from the main road to Brooklyn. To reach it, Mason had to drive straight through town, and he did so without looking either to the left or right. He sat rigidly straight, his hands tight on the wheel as he tried to avoid accidents. He came close to having one at a red light when he forgot for a moment that he was supposed to stop, and another time when the car in front of him failed to signal for a turn.

A bicyclist had come closer to becoming an accident statistic than the others because Mason didn't see him in the lane of traffic until it was nearly too late. Mason swerved to his left, almost hitting a taxi, and the driver's honking and animated gestures let Mason know what the man thought of him. The bicyclist was equally complimentary, and Mason was glad when he had left him behind.

When he arrived safely at the great pile of wood and stone that was Derlicht Haus, Mason stopped the car at the curb and gave a sigh of relief. He had gotten there without killing himself or anyone else, and he was grateful for that.

He got out of the car, and the cold north wind hit him, pulling at his coat and flapping his pants legs. He hurried up the walk and up the steps to the porch. The light was on, and Antonia must have been waiting for him, because even before he could ring the bell, the door opened and she was standing there in the hallway.

She was even prettier than he had remembered. Her thick black hair shone in the light, and her eyes sparkled with greeting.

"Come in," she said. "It's freezing out there."

Mason wasted no time in entering, and Antonia closed the door behind him.

"I'm so glad you could come," Antonia said, taking

his coat and hanging it in a convenient closet. "I think we got off on the wrong foot this morning, and I want to start over. I really do want us to become friends."

If he had been a silver-tongued devil, Mason would have said he hoped they could become more than friends, but as it was he just said, "Uh, me too."

"My father would like to meet you," Antonia said. "He's right down the hall."

Mason didn't think he wanted to meet Frederick Derlicht, not if his reaction to Mason was going to be anything like James's reaction when Mason had told him where he was going.

"To see a Derlicht?" James had said. "You must be out of your mind."

Which was about what Mason had expected him to say.

"It's a Derlicht woman," Mason said. "You want me to meet women. You want me to get married. Antonia would be perfect for me."

Laura was nowhere around. If she had been, it was possible that James might not have made his next statement.

"There is no perfect woman."

Mason didn't want to argue. He said, "I meant she's perfect for me. She lives in town, she knows about our family ..."

"What do you mean she knows our family?"

James's voice was sharp, and Mason felt defensive.

"She knows about our history. She mentioned Benjamin Noir to me today."

"And that's another thing," James said. "I don't like it

that you slipped away to meet her without letting me know."

"I would have, but I was afraid you'd act the way you are now. There's no need for you to be hostile to her. You don't even know her."

James didn't rise to the bait. He said, "I told you to find a wife, not a proven enemy of our family. I'd rather you go back to your work if this is what you call dating."

"I, well, after yesterday I didn't feel like facing the monitor. And then I met Antonia."

Mason had not mentioned the episodes in the basement, and he didn't intend to.

"I can understand that. You'll get over it. I hope your avoidance of work has nothing to do with this Derlicht woman."

"You'd like her if you met her. She's very scholarly."

"I doubt that I would like her. I never met a Derlicht that I liked."

"Which ones have you met?"

"Never mind that. I hope you don't plan to marry this woman."

Mason thought it wouldn't be a bad idea if he did, but he knew it wouldn't be wise to belabor the point. So he said, "I just met her."

James nodded. "You could get into a lot of trouble if you stayed around her too much. I told you that things were going on around you here, that there are forces that are moving because of you. These forces haven't become dynamic on their own. There's something calling them to action."

"Nothing is going on," Mason said, trying to keep his

voice level and not succeeding. "I haven't seen any evidence of dynamic forces."

"You can keep on telling yourself that as much as you want," James said, "but that won't change the facts. You should just admit what you've experienced and learn from it."

Mason didn't see what there was to learn, and he didn't want to discuss it. To do so, he would have had to admit that the experiences were real. He told his father that he was leaving, and went to get the car.

Frederick Derlicht was nothing like James at all. He was as cordial as Mason could have hoped, smiling as if he wouldn't mind having Mason as a son-in-law, and the sooner, the better.

"It is a pleasure to meet you, Mason," he said, offering his hand.

They shook hands, and Mason told Frederick that it was a pleasure to meet him as well.

"My daughter tells me that you are interested in your family history," Frederick said.

Mason looked at Antonia, who avoided his gaze by looking at her father.

"I don't really know much about my family," Mason said. "But I was hoping to tell her what I could to help her with her Special Project."

"I'm sure you will be able to do so. Both she and I appreciate it. Now if you will excuse me ..."

"Sure," Mason said, and Frederick left the room.

Mason stood there wondering what to do next. It

wasn't every evening that he found himself alone with a woman, much less a beautiful one.

Antonia was hesitant as well, but for different reasons. She didn't want to frighten Mason away again, but at the same time she wanted to let him know that there were serious issues for them to discuss. Probably the best way, she decided was to give Mason another chance to talk about his work with computers and hope he would be more willing than he had that morning to do so.

"Why don't we have something to drink?" she asked.

"Fine," Mason said. "But I really don't like to drink. I like to keep my mind clear."

"I was thinking of coffee or a soda."

"Oh. Coffee would be fine."

"Great. I'll make some."

"Cool," Mason said.

They both liked to read, they both liked coffee. Perfect. He'd known it all along.

They sat in the kitchen and drank black French roast, which was the type of coffee Mason preferred.

Antonia was charming and friendly, and she encouraged Mason to talk about his work. To his surprise, he found himself telling her all about MIND-NET, something that he had never discussed with anyone outside his own family. Even the people he communicated with electronically knew only bits and pieces of what he was attempting.

Antonia did not have to pretend fascination with what Mason was telling her. She realized that Mason, without even being aware of it, was quite possibly sitting on a research gold mine, at least from her point of view. A computer has files, and if a person's psyche could somehow be paged through like a file, the very roots of how urban legends got started might be discovered. If Mason's experiments bore fruit and he allowed her to use his work, she might become the world's foremost authority on her chosen topic.

"I'm probably boring you," Mason said when he had run out of things to say. "It's all pretty technical."

"You weren't boring me at all. I think you're doing amazing work. I wish there were some way I could help you with it."

Mason sipped his coffee, grimaced at the lukewarm flavor.

"I came over here to help you," he said, thinking that she was just being polite. "I seem to have forgotten all about that and talked about myself too much. You wanted to know about my family."

"Only if you want to talk about it. I can see why you might be hesitant. Some strange things are happening around here."

Mason didn't like the sound of that.

"What do you mean?" he asked.

Antonia hadn't really meant to tell Mason about the apparition she had seen that day, but she thought he deserved to know. Besides, she thought, it might get him to open up about his family.

"I saw someone today," she said.

There was nothing unusual in that statement, but it made Mason uncomfortable, considering his sightings of Thomas, imagined though they were.

"Who did you see?" he asked. "Somebody I should know?"

"I think you should. He looked a lot like you."

Mason got up from his seat and walked around the table in an attempt to conceal his agitation.

"Did he say anything to you?" he asked.

"He said he was sorry for bumping into me, but it wasn't his fault. I was the one who bumped into him."

Mason felt a little better. You couldn't bump into a ghost.

"I hope you didn't hurt him," he said.

"Oh, I didn't really bump him. I just came close."

Mason's chest felt hollow. "And that's all he had to say?"

"Yes." Antonia thought she might as well go one step further. "Have you ever heard the stories about ghosts here in Geiststadt?"

Mason hardly trusted himself to speak, but he managed to say that he had without having his voice crack.

"Have you ever seen them?" Antonia asked.

Mason wanted to run. He was sweating, and everything in him was straining for the exit. But he said, "I don't believe in ghosts."

Antonia wondered why Mason seemed so agitated. She said, "I didn't mean to make you uncomfortable."

"I'm not uncomfortable," Mason said, lying through his teeth. "I just don't like talking about ghosts. It's silly."

"No, it's not. I think the one I saw was related to you. I think it was Jonathan Noir."

Mason went back to the table and sat down.

"Jonathan? Not Thomas?"

Antonia remembered his reaction to Thomas's name at their first meeting.

"No, I'm sure it wasn't Thomas. He and Jonathan were twins, so both of them might have a family resemblance to you."

"It seems you know a lot more about my family than I do."

"I've learned a few things." Now that Mason had calmed down a bit, Antonia decided to push him a little more. "I've been reading some old handwritten accounts about my own family, and yours as well. One of them was written a long time ago, right after Jonathan's death. He...would you like to see it?"

"The book?"

"Yes. I think you should know more about your family."

"I was supposed to be telling you about them, not the other way around."

"I seem to know more than you do, and I'm the one who saw Jonathan. So, do you want to have a look?"

Antonia thought it would be an interesting experiment to find out whether Mason could read the book or if the words would be mere swirls without meaning in his eyes.

Mason wasn't sure he wanted to see anything. The talk about Thomas and Jonathan was making him nervous, and the way Antonia talked so matter-of-factly about having seen a ghost did more than make him nervous.

It scared him.

Oh, he knew there were no ghosts, he had convinced himself of that, but Antonia seemed to take them for granted. That kind of attitude wasn't something he was looking for in a wife. He was going to have to convince her that there were no ghosts before their relationship went much further. And he did hope it would go further. Just being with her gave him a feeling of happiness of a kind he'd never experienced before, and he didn't want it to end.

"Well?" Antonia said.

"I'd like to see the books," Mason said.

CHAPTER TWENTY

Antonia didn't think to ask her father about the wisdom of showing Mason the books or taking him to the attic, nor did she think how Agatha's undying enmity for the Noirs might be affected by a visit by one of the modern generation of that family. Instead, she took Mason's hand and led him up the stairway that took them to the upper stories of the house.

Mason's skin tingled at her touch. He hadn't held hands with anyone since...well, he couldn't remember. That might have explained why he didn't notice how cold it seemed to be getting as they went higher up the stairs.

Antonia didn't think about the cold, either. She was too excited about showing Mason the books and seeing if he could read them to notice.

When she opened the door to the attic, however, she could feel the change. The wind, which had been strong before, was now howling around the eaves, and it seemed to be finding cracks in the attic walls that hadn't existed before. When Antonia turned on the light, Mason could see ripples of dust rising along the floor.

"I hope you're not too sensitive to dust and dirt," Antonia said, stifling a sneeze of her own.

"It doesn't bother me," Mason said.

What bothered him was the creaking of the walls. It almost seemed that the old house was swaying in the high wind.

"Here are the books," Antonia said, leading him to the table where they lay.

She let go of Mason's hand and reached for the cover of the larger book. It slid away from her, to the farther edge of the table.

She reached for the smaller one. It flew up into the air and disappeared with an audible *pop* that could be heard even above the noise of the wind and the creaking of the house.

"Damn," Antonia said. "Did you see that?"

Mason had seen it, all right, and he had heard it, too. He didn't like it one bit. He especially didn't like it that both he and Antonia had seen it, which would make it much harder to explain away.

A scritchy, scratchy noise caught his attention, and he looked across the room to see spiders, fat black spiders, pouring out of the cracks in the walls and the baseboard. Hundreds of them. Thousands.

"Jesus," Mason said.

Antonia turned and saw the spiders.

"I don't think Jesus has anything to do with it," she said. "Let's get out of here."

That seemed like a great idea to Mason. He took her hand and started toward the door.

It slammed shut as if pushed by a giant invisible hand.

That can't be good, Mason thought.

He released Antonia's hand and ran across the room to the door. He turned the knob and pulled. For all that he accomplished, he might as well have been pulling a boulder the size of New Jersey.

He looked back at the spiders. They were moving swiftly across the room. Soon they would be at the table that held the remaining book. Antonia still stood beside it, unmoving.

"Antonia," Mason said.

She didn't seem to hear, and it was then that Mason noticed that the wind was blowing harder.

Not outside. In the room itself. And the temperature had dropped so rapidly he could see his breath whirl in steaming clouds seconds before the wind whisked it away. His clothing flapped around him, and he felt like a scarecrow.

"Antonia!" he called, louder this time.

Her eyes focused on him, and she started to walk forward just as the infestation of spiders swarmed up the legs of the table and the chair that was nearby. They covered the top of the table like a living black cloth, and they covered the book like a mass of black ashes. There seemed to be more of them every second, as if they were somehow multiplying right there in the room, instantaneously.

Antonia had moved away from them, and she was halfway to Mason by that time.

As long as they stay on the table, we'll be fine, Mason thought. He couldn't help remembering the spit spider that Thomas Noir had put on his chest. Was this more of his handiwork? A reminder of his power?

Of course the spiders didn't stay on the table. Or maybe they did. There were so many of them now that it was impossible to tell if the ones on the table had moved, or if a thousand more had materialized out of nowhere. The floor was carpeted with them.

Antonia went past Mason to the door, but she had no more luck in opening it than he had. It was an immovable object.

"What are we going to do?" Antonia asked.

The wind whipped her hair around her face, and she brushed it aside.

It was odd, Mason thought, that the wind had no effect on the spiders. It should have blown them aside like dry leaves, but they continued their inexorable march toward Mason and Antonia.

"Step on them?" Mason said.

"I don't think it would work. And there are too many of them."

"Call an exterminator?"

Antonia laughed, and the sound made Mason feel good. Too bad he didn't feel as clever as he thought he sounded, because the spiders were only a couple of feet away from them and the wind was howling. The entire attic was shaking.

Mason and Antonia backed against the door. The spiders now surrounded them, covering the floor in a semi-circle in front of them and the wall behind them. Mason pushed Antonia behind him.

"This is my fault," Antonia said. She had to yell to be

heard above the sound of the wind. "I should never have brought you here."

Somehow Mason found himself putting his arms around her. She melted against him, and for a fraction of a second he forgot all about the spiders.

Then they covered his shoes, and he remembered them. He tried to make another witty remark, but he found that his voice was stuck in his throat. He had never liked spiders.

When they started up his legs, he found his voice again, but what came out was not a witty remark. It was more like a whimper. "Stop them!" he managed to say.

"I don't know how," Antonia said. She shuddered against his body.

He was too filled with horror and disgust to look down, but he knew the spiders were on her legs, too.

When they passed his socks he could feel their tiny sticky legs on his own, and his voice came back in full cry as his arms tightened around Antonia.

She didn't cry out at all, but her body was no longer cringing. She had gone rigid.

Mason wanted to faint and escape at least the feeling of the legs creeping up him, but he could not. The spiders continued their implacable march upward.

Why hadn't they bitten him yet? Jesus, were they waiting until they got to his testicles?

The entire room seethed with spiders. There was not a vacant inch of space on the walls, the floor, or the ceiling. Even Mason's clothing was covered with the quivering creatures.

An iron band tightened around Mason's chest, and he

could hardly breathe. No matter what he told himself about this, he would not be able to pass it off as imaginary.

He could see the spiders, and he could feel the spiders. He could even *smell* the spiders.

He knew they were going to kill him unless he did something about them, but there was nothing he could do.

Or maybe there was. He could use some of that *heka* his father had told him about. He was, after all, the thirteenth son of a thirteenth son of a Noir, and there was supposed to be power in that. It was time he found out the truth of it, if not for his own sake, for Antonia's.

He reached deep into the recesses of his mind, far back beyond the rational part that he so cultivated and admired to places he had never been except in dreams. He found something there, a spark, a light, a fire, and he brought it out into the open. It hung in the middle of the air and flared, there in the attic of Derlicht Haus. The wind buffeted it, and it almost disappeared. Mason strained his mental capacities to their fullest, concentrating on the flame and forgetting everything else.

It was as if he was standing alone on a great, barren plain. The sun was burning down, a great ball of fire in the sky. Mason stared at the sun, and his eyes, instead of being blinded, glowed with a fire of their own, and flames began to drop from the sun to fall on the arid ground.

Mason heard a crackling noise and looked again. He no longer saw the sun. Instead he saw that a fire was burning the spiders. It had started in the middle of the room and was spreading outward toward the walls, racing along the floor faster than even the spiders had run as it consumed them, leaving nothing behind, not even ash. It sped up the walls and onto the ceiling, and Mason braced himself as the flames ran up his legs, covering him and Antonia in a fiery haze, but he felt no heat or pain. The fire passed up over his head and vanished into the air.

Mason stood there, unable to move until Antonia stirred in his arms.

"What happened?" she said.

"I'm not sure," Mason told her. "What do you think happened."

"Spiders happened."

Mason didn't want to admit it.

"We could have imagined it."

"Both of us imagining the same thing? I don't think so."

Mason didn't really think so, either. But he hoped so.

"If we didn't imagine it," he said, "where are the spiders now?"

"The fire burned them. A fire without heat," she said.

"Where did the fire come from?" Mason asked, more afraid, in some ways, of the answer than he had been of the spiders.

"I think it came from us," she said.

Mason didn't think she could have imagined the fire if he'd only imagined that he'd created it. The thought might have elated someone else, someone who craved power of a certain kind, but it depressed Mason. He didn't want that kind of power, didn't even want to be associated with it. His father might be pleased, more than pleased, but for Mason it was more of a defeat than a victory.

"Where did the spiders come from?" he asked.

"I've had a feeling all along that I was being watched here," Antonia said. "I've seen several spiders. But never that many."

She hadn't answered Mason's question, but he didn't press her. She might not have known the answer anyway.

It was only then that Mason realized he was still holding her. It seemed natural to him, though he had so little experience with women that nothing about holding one was natural.

But he didn't let go. Antonia didn't seem to mind.

"The book and the table weren't burned," she said, and Mason looked at them for the first time since the fire.

"The chair's there, too," he pointed out.

For that matter, there was no smell of burning in the room, and there was no smoke. The temperature was cool, but not cold, and there was no wind blowing through the walls as there had been only a short time before. The walls, the floor, and the ceiling were just as dusty as they had been before, not scorched at all by the fire that had spread across them.

Mason mentioned these things to Antonia and added, "So maybe we did imagine it. All of it."

"No," she said. "We didn't."

And Mason believed her.

Antonia put her head back down on Mason's shoulder, her mind racing. She'd *felt* Mason focus his mind, felt his intention to burn the spiders but not the room, and not them. Instinctively, she, too, stretched out her mind and what she—*felt?saw?touched?*—astounded her.

Her mind was much stronger than Mason's.

It had been his intention, but her strength that burned the spiders without heat. Her mind, not his.

He was pulling her towards the door, wanting to leave, and for a moment, she thought about telling him what she'd experienced. But a voice in her mind, strong and feminine, said no.

Better to let him believe it was him than to give away your strength.

And whatever or whoever that voice was, Antonia decided, was right.

CHAPTER TWENTY-ONE

B y the next morning, Mason was a nervous wreck. He couldn't explain *why* he felt the way he did, but there was no denying that in a matter of a couple meetings, he'd fallen in love with Antonia. There was also not much use in denying that there were things about himself and his family that he did not understand in the least. His whole view of the world had changed overnight.

He no longer doubted that Thomas Noir was trying to reach him. He didn't know why Thomas believed that MIND-NET could be sped up, but he knew it wouldn't be healthy, not if what Antonia had told him last night was true.

He was ready to admit that everything he had previously dismissed as being the result of stress had in fact happened. It wasn't easy to adjust, but Mason was making the effort.

After the episode with the spiders and the fire, Mason and Antonia had gone back downstairs to a study located on the ground floor of Derlicht Haus. Antonia had laid claim to the room as her own territory when she started graduate school. It was cluttered with papers and books, not in any particular order that Mason could see, and on the desk there was a pad of lined yellow pages lying beside a Sony laptop. It was this pad that Antonia picked up and referred to when she began telling him about his family.

After she had finished recounting all that she had read and surmised, Mason was dumbfounded. He had never heard the story of Jonathan's sacrifice, and in fact Jonathan had always been described as more or less of a villain in the Noir family, when he was mentioned at all.

"Surely you know that his ghost appears in Geiststadt occasionally," Antonia had said. "Usually when someone is having some kind of bad situation. There were quite a few sightings after the World Trade Center bombing, for example. Quite a few families here lost relatives or friends there."

Mason had heard those tales, but he had disregarded them. Until now they had seemed ridiculous. If there was any truth in the stories, Mason wondered why Jonathan had returned just at this time. There had been trouble aplenty in the world in the last few years besides the destruction of the World Trade Center: the disaster with the Space Shuttle Columbia, the new war in the Middle East, nuclear threats from all over. But it didn't seem likely that a Noir ghost would be coming around because of those global troubles. He would be here because of something in Geiststadt.

Or maybe it was just that people saw visions of ghosts

when they were under stress. That would be a much more logical explanation.

Mason, however, no longer believed that logical explanations were necessarily the correct ones.

"Don't you see?" Antonia had said. "Terrible things happened in your family, and in mine, because of some kind of struggle for power between Jonathan and Thomas. Now they're back. What could they be looking for?"

Mason already knew. He could tell Antonia without risking too much.

"MIND-NET. Thomas has been quite clear about it, though Jonathan seems intent on stopping him."

Antonia hadn't agreed. "Why would he be interested in MIND-NET? What good could it possibly do a ghost?"

"Thomas wants to return, not as a ghost but as a person. If what you're saying is true, he was more or less confined to Noir Manor for most of his life. Now he wants to enjoy the world as only someone human can. MIND-NET could be the instrument."

"But he was behind the murders. He's a killer, or if he isn't, the killings were done at his instigation."

That story had not been a part of Mason's upbringing, either, and he hated to believe it. And why should he? The Derlichts had never liked Mason's family, and Antonia was getting all her information from Derlicht history.

Even at that, however, Mason found that he did believe. He was believing all sorts of things that only a day or so earlier had seemed preposterous to him. Either he was going crazy, or the things that he had always believed to be true were only a part of the truth rather than its entirety. He suspected that the latter was the case.

"I just wish there were some way to prove all this once and for all," he said.

Antonia suggested a test.

"We can go to the old Dutch cemetery," she said. "That's where the Geiststadt ghosts are supposed to be the most likely to appear. We'll go there calmly, like people conducting an experiment. We can take a boom-box with some soothing music, strictly anti-spooky stuff. We can even take some drinks."

Mason remembered his father having said much the same thing about the old cemetery, but that had not impressed Mason.

"I used to go there now and then," he told Antonia. "I never saw any ghosts."

"How long ago was that?"

Mason thought about it. "Twenty years or so, I think."

"And you haven't been back since then?"

"I didn't have a reason."

"Now you do. Things have changed. You're different. The situation is different. What could it hurt to go and see what happens?"

"Not tonight," Mason said. "I've had about all the spookiness I can stand for one day."

Antonia had seen the wisdom of that, but she had insisted that they meet the next afternoon and go to the cemetery.

"Not too late. We don't even have to be there after dark."

"Ghosts don't come out until dark," Mason said.

Antonia just looked at him.

"All right, I guess they can come out any time they want to."

"That's right. So I'll see you tomorrow afternoon?"

Mason had agreed. He wanted to see her again, no matter what the situation. If he had to visit an old cemetery, then that's what he would do.

Now, however, thinking it over as he sat in the sunlight that poured into the library of Noir Manor, it seemed like a foolish idea. He was trying to think of an excuse not to go when his father came into the room.

"Well?" James said.

"Well, what?"

"Well, what happened last night?"

Mason didn't want to talk about that to anyone, least of all to his father, but he owed James that much. So he told him an edited version of the evening's events, leaving out the story of Thomas Noir's role in the murders, and the death of Agatha in the fire, but mentioning the spiders and what had happened to them.

After Mason was finished, James said, "The Derlichts have had a grudge against us for centuries. You should never have gone there. You're lucky to be alive."

"You mean you believe what I just told you?"

"Of course. I told you that you had *heka*. It's taken you a long time to use it, but it's always been present. It's good that you finally gave in to the power inside you. The Derlichts fear it, and they fear you. So they tried to destroy you."

"I don't think so. Antonia likes me, and her father seemed nice enough."

"The Derlichts have always been good at hiding their feelings. Don't tell me you got through the entire evening without someone trying to degrade our family."

"I talked mostly to Antonia."

"And what's that supposed to mean?"

Mason didn't feel that Antonia had been degrading anyone. She had been reporting what she believed to be the facts.

"It means that she didn't say anything to make me think less of the family. And she did a pretty good job of proving that things I've been dismissing as hallucinations are real."

"I suppose I owe her some thanks for that. At least it got you to use the power you've always possessed. But I can't help thinking there's more to the story."

Sometimes it seemed that James could read Mason's mind. In light of what Mason was finding out about the family, it wasn't beyond the realm of possibility.

"Well?" James said. "Is there anything else you want to tell me?"

"I'm still one experiment away from absolute conviction," Mason said.

"What kind of experiment could that be?"

"Antonia and I are going to the old Dutch cemetery this afternoon. If any ghosts show up, I'll have to admit that I've been wrong all along."

"Oh, the ghosts will be there. They always are. Whether they reveal themselves to you or not is another story. Now tell me more about this Antonia Derlicht."

Mason tried to pretend that, while he and Antonia had

gotten along just fine, there was nothing more to their friendship than an interest in their family histories.

James saw through the pose with ease. "You like her more than that. Are you in love with her?"

"No, of course not. I've only met her a couple of times."

James gave Mason a shrewd look. "There's no use in trying to fool me, Mason. I'm your father, and I'm a Noir."

"Then let's just say that I could be in love if I knew what love was. I'm not sure I do."

James rubbed his bony chin. "I don't think it would be for the best if a member of our family married a Derlicht. In fact, it could be a disaster."

"I'm not planning to marry her," Mason said, and realized to his surprise that it was a lie.

"We'll see, I suppose. What do you propose to do if your expedition this afternoon is a success?"

"For one thing, I'll have to admit that it was Thomas who somehow drew me into the computer monitor."

"I told you that to begin with."

Mason still hadn't told James about the incident with the computer in the lab or the TV set, and he didn't intend to do so.

"I know. And it looks as if you were right. If you were, I'll have to do some serious considering about what to do with MIND-NET."

"You can't stop your work. It's far too important."

But I can't let Thomas get his ghostly hands on it, either, Mason thought.

"We'll see," he said.

CHAPTER TWENTY-TWO

D o you speak any German?" Antonia asked.

She and Mason were on their way to the old cemetery. He had driven to her house again, doing a little better than he had the night before, but they were walking to the cemetery, which lay to the north and east of Derlicht Haus.

There had been a time in Geiststadt when practically everyone spoke German, at least in the home. Even in the middle of the twentieth century, most of the population was bilingual. But in the latter half of the century, most people had begun to lose interest in their heritage and considered themselves strictly Americans. Now German was a course that was taught in the better public schools, not a living language for the majority of Geiststadt residents.

"No," Mason said. "I don't speak German. I can read it, but that's all. Why?"

"Because we're going to look for ghosts, and the very name of Geiststadt should tell us that we'll find them."

"Ghost Town," Mason said. "Spirit Town. I've always known what the name meant, but I never really thought much about the connection to the old stories. Do you mean that ghosts have been seen here since the founding of the town?"

It had been a beautiful day when they started out hiking up on the ridge beyond Derlicht Haus. There was a bite in the air, but with a cloudless blue sky gave them a hint that spring might not be too far away. Now, however, Mason noticed that clouds were gathering in the sky, and they had already obscured the sun. The temperature had dropped noticeably. Now Mason wished they had brought a thermos of coffee.

"The original name of the town was Dunkelstad," Antonia told him. "So there were no ghosts here at first. But the name was changed for some reason. Maybe for a good reason."

"What about HangedMan's Hill? Since you're the historian here, tell me where that name came from."

They could see the hill from where they stood, and Mason had always assumed some kind of criminal must have been hanged there. But he had been wrong.

"It's a name from the Revolutionary War days," Antonia said. "The Battle of Brooklyn was fought a few miles from here, but before that a troop of Hessian soldiers rode through Geiststadt. For some reason, they attacked the town. No one knows why, since they were from the same kind of background as the residents. But no matter what the reason was, they sacked the town. They might have destroyed it completely, but a militia raised from the surrounding towns surprised them before they could finish the job. Most of them got away, but those who didn't...well, that's how HangedMan's Hill got its name."

The story was grislier than Mason had expected it to be. The bloodshed in and around Geiststadt went back a long way.

"No wonder people talk about ghosts around here," Mason said.

"There's more to the stories than that, I believe. There are some places on the earth that gather power to them, and power attracts power. I have a feeling that Geiststadt is a place like that. I suspect that's why my ancestors chose to settle here. And yours as well."

Mason hadn't thought of it that way, but it made sense. Or it did now. A day earlier he would have laughed at the idea, but he wasn't the same person he'd been then.

"What about the White Lady?" he asked. "Isn't she supposed to haunt the cemetery?"

Antonia laughed. "Another urban legend. I've never seen her, but maybe today will be the time that I do."

"Do you know the origin of that story?"

"No, but I'd like to find out. It would make a great addition to the paper I'm writing."

They continued their walk until they reached the top of the ridge. The view was spectacular, even without the sun, which was now entirely blanketed by the clouds. The town of Geiststadt was spread out for them to see, and Mason could almost imagine what it must have looked like a couple of hundred years ago, with narrow muddy streets and only two great buildings with smoke rising from their chimneys, the homes of the Derlichts and the Noirs. Now it was hard to make the two houses out in the welter of paved streets and modern buildings of brick and steel that had risen all around the town, but the Mill Pond still glittered like a silver mirror in the center as it had since near the beginnings of Geiststadt.

Mason and Antonia did not comment on the sight. They simply enjoyed it. Then they turned to the cemetery, which lay within a waist-high iron fence rusted to a color that reminded Mason of dried blood.

The graves inside the fence had not been well kept up, for hardly anyone visited the cemetery these days, and no one still living in Geiststadt had ancestors buried there. Weeds grew thickly, and most of the old gravestones, which had been none too sturdy to begin with, had fallen over. Those that were standing were so worn by time and weather that the inscriptions were almost impossible to distinguish. Mason had been told that some of the earliest graves were marked only with wooden crosses, but if that was true, no trace of the crosses remained.

"It looks old," Mason said, "but it doesn't look haunted."

"How does a haunted place look?" said Antonia.

"I don't know. Not like this."

"You don't feel anything?"

"No, not a thing except the wind. It's cold."

There hadn't been much of a wind when they'd started out, but now it stirred the weeds in the cemetery and blew Antonia's hair across her face.

"If I didn't know better, I'd think it was nearly evening," Mason said.

He looked at his watch. It was only three o'clock. It was still a long time until evening.

Antonia tugged at the sleeve of his jacket, and they

189

walked inside the cemetery gateway. The gate itself had fallen open years ago and now hung at a slant against the fence, one of its hinges completely rusted away and the other barely connecting the gate to the fence.

"Now what?" Mason asked when they were about in the center of the cemetery.

Antonia smiled and took his hand.

"Now we wait for the ghosts," she said.

Mason smiled back at her. In spite of the wind and the cold, he felt happy to be there. He felt comfortable with Antonia, and he had not experienced anything like that with another person for longer than he could remember. His parents were different. He felt all right with them, but it wasn't the same.

"What if the ghosts don't cooperate?" he asked.

"Then we'll just have to go home. But let's give them some time."

Mason didn't mind. He would have waited there forever as long as Antonia stayed with him.

They stood in silence, waiting.

Mason wasn't sure how much time had passed. He had lost track of it, falling into one of his daydreams, this time about himself and Antonia and what life would be like if they were married. He found it hard to think of himself as a husband, and maybe even a father, but he discovered that he liked the idea, and that was as much a surprise to him as it would have been to his own family.

He remembered what it had been like to grow up in a large family of brothers. He recalled family football games, some of which had been pretty rough and tumble, and going to the beach in the summers. It was a little like traveling with the circus. Or at least with the clowns.

He wondered if Antonia had ever thought about having a large family of her own. His parents, of course, had made it clear that they expected it of him, and they wanted him to get started as soon as possible, though Antonia wasn't going to make his father happy as Mason's wife.

James wasn't the one who mattered, however, and Mason was going to be the one who made the decision when it came to marriage.

"Do you hear them?" Antonia said, breaking into his thoughts.

Mason twitched as he came out of his reverie. He didn't hear anything.

"Who?" he asked, looking around. He didn't see anyone except Antonia.

"Listen," Antonia told him.

Mason stood quietly doing as she had said. He heard the sound of the wind, the rustling of the weeds, and the far-off call of some kind of bird. There was another rustling as well, but after a few seconds he realized that it wasn't an external sound.

It was in his head. As if his head was hollow and the wind was blowing inside of it.

"I hear *something*," he said.

"Hush. Listen."

Mason listened, and the sound that he had thought was the wind in his skull changed to something else, still sibilant, but different. Like whispering.

"Voices," he said. "Inside my head."

"Yes. Don't talk. Listen."

As the voices became clearer, Mason tried to figure out what they were saying. It seemed to him that they were speaking nonsense, and while he could make out something that might have been words, he had no idea what they meant.

He looked around the cemetery. The clouds were so thick that it was dark as midnight. Far away across the ridge, the edges of the clouds were rimmed by silvery light, and the sun was shining still on Geiststadt and the Mill Pond. Darkness enveloped the cemetery, but the town itself was unaffected.

A corner of the cemetery began to glow, as if someone had lit a fire there. It *was* a fire, Mason thought, but nothing was being consumed by it. In the middle of the flames, something moved.

It was nothing more than a black shape at first, but then it resolved itself to the figure of a man in a uniform. Mason knew, though he could not have explained how, that the uniform was that of a Hessian soldier.

The man was joined by others. Mason did not count them, but there were a dozen or more, all of them standing in the flames, all of them speaking to Mason in his head in the language he did not understand. It sounded like German.

Mason's hand tightened on Antonia's. She did not look at him.

One of the soldiers walked in advance of the others, and the voices in Mason's head gradually became one voice. Mason still could not make out the individual words, but he didn't suppose that mattered. If he had ever wondered about the existence of ghosts in Geiststadt, he didn't wonder any longer. The ghosts were there, they were real, and they were speaking to him across the centuries.

The soldier stopped walking, and the others behind him stopped as well. Mason could see now that their uniforms were ripped and torn and that their bodies were covered with wounds. The blood on their clothing, faces, and hair looked as fresh as if it had just been spilled.

The soldier's eyes, Mason noticed, were not eyes at all, merely hollow black sockets rimmed with blood. Yet Mason felt that the man could see him.

Mason sneaked a look at Antonia. She was staring straight ahead, and Mason wondered if she could understand what the soldier was saying. If so, she gave no sign of it.

The sound in Mason's head ceased. The soldier raised a hand in what might have been either a gesture of greeting or farewell and turned back to the flame that still burned behind him. The other men stepped aside; he passed between them and disappeared into the fire. When he was gone, his men, without a glance in Mason's direction, turned and followed him. The fire blazed higher then, and for a moment, Mason thought the show was over.

But a new figure was emerging from the flames.

Antonia saw the dog creature step through the portal of flame and for several long seconds, she simply stared at it, frozen to the ground like a statue, with her mouth

193

hanging open. Her mind spun in a long, downward spiral as she tried to grasp what she was seeing, think what, if anything she should do.

The same strong, feminine voice she'd heard in her head, in the attic, said, *It's Anubis, the Egyptian God of the Dead. Or his avatar. Most mortals are powerless against him. You are not.*

What can I possibly do against that? Antonia asked the voice.

Focus your thoughts, girl. Anubis himself, if he actually exists, cannot materialize in this realm. He's a dog and his interest is in the dead. Throw him a bone.

The Hessians! Antonia thought. She looked over at Mason, who was standing there, rooted to the ground just as she had been.

"Mason," she said.

No reply. His eyes were glazed over in shock.

"Mason!" she repeated, nudging him in the ribs. "Help me!"

He blinked several times, and Antonia could see that his hands were shaking. "I...I can't," he stammered. "He's come for me."

"What?"

"Anubis," he hissed. "He's Thomas' watchdog or something."

Tell him to open his mind to you, the voice in her head whispered.

Antonia obeyed instantly, repeating the instructions to Mason.

"Oh... okay," Mason said, sounding as though he'd been drugged.

Nonetheless, she felt his mind creak open. Anubis was walking towards her now, his mouth open in a doggy-grin, his muscles outlined in fine detail.

She stepped forward to meet him, standing in front of Mason. "What do you want?" she asked.

Anubis pointed. At Mason.

Antonia shook her head. "No," she said. "You cannot have him. He is not dead, not part of your domain." She didn't know where the words were coming from, but they were there when she needed them.

Anubis made a high-pitched yipping sound, and pointed again.

"No," Antonia repeated. "You seek the dead, not the living." She gestured at the fire portal. "They went there."

Anubis turned to look into the flaring portal, turned back to her.

"You have no power here, Anubis. Go find the Hessians or return to your own realm. This man is not yours."

A long second passed, stretched into two, while Anubis cocked his head as though listening to instructions only he could hear. Finally, he made his high-pitched yipping noise again, though this time it sounded more like laughter than anything else. He turned and walked back towards the portal. As he neared it, an idea occurred to Antonia, and she called out to the dog creature, who stopped and turned his head back towards her.

"Tell your master, Thomas, that Mason Noir belongs to me, Antonia Derlicht. That he's under my protection."

Anubis laughed again, shrugged, and as he stepped through the portal, Antonia unleashed the power in her mind like a fist. It slammed into Anubis' back and he stumbled forward through the portal, which flickered and flared once more, before going out completely.

That will give him something to think about! the voice in her head said.

Let's hope so, Antonia thought, then turned back to Mason, who was still rooted to the ground like a tree. *Maybe this will be a dream to him,* she hoped.

The fire was gone. The portal that the Hessian soldiers had come through had vanished without a trace. The weeds stood just as green as they had before it had appeared. Mason shook his head. For a second, it had felt like he'd just woken from a dream. The images flittered through his mind and he tried to grasp hold of them, but they fell apart in wisps before he could grab on to them.

The weather was changing again. The thick black clouds that had covered the sun were thinning rapidly, like inferior paper coming apart in a rushing stream. Within a couple of minutes the sun was shining through the tatters, and it was as if the darkness and the fire and the ghosts had never been.

Mason relaxed his grip on Antonia's hand, which he realized now he'd been holding on to, and she looked at him.

"I think that should do away any doubts you might have had," she said. "There are ghosts in Geiststadt, and the supernatural is as real as anything else. That is, you'll believe that if you saw what I saw."

"What did you see?"

Antonia described the exact scene that Mason had witnessed. There was no way she could have done so had she not seen it, just as he had. He was convinced now, though he didn't want to be, that everything he'd been told by his father and by Antonia was true.

There was only one question left unanswered: what was he going to do about it?

He didn't know.

CHAPTER TWENTY-THREE

Antonia didn't know what she was going to do, either. Something had happened to her, something that she had not counted on.

She had fallen in love with Mason Noir. Suddenly and without warning.

Antonia couldn't explain why. Mason had a lot of things wrong with him from her point of view. He was clumsy, he was introverted, and he was a Noir. Until yesterday, he had dogmatically insisted that there was no such thing as occult knowledge, and even after having suffered through the attack of the spiders, he hadn't wanted to believe what had happened until he had more proof. Yet, while he doubted, he had also tried to protect her. Maybe that was what love was all about, she thought. You loved someone in spite of what you perceived as his shortcomings.

At any rate, she had given him proof enough of the occult and the supernatural. She hadn't even been certain herself that the ghosts would appear in the Dutch cemetery, but they had, and even Mason couldn't deny it. She counted it lucky that he didn't seem to recall any of the episode with Anubis.

Their visit to the cemetery had been almost twenty-four hours ago. Afterward, she and Mason had returned to her house with hardly a word passing between them. But they hadn't needed words. She knew perfectly well how he felt about what had happened. She knew perfectly well how he felt about her, too, and perhaps he sensed something of her feelings also.

When Mason left Derlicht Haus later that evening, they both knew that some kind of line had been crossed, but as for Antonia, she didn't know exactly what that meant. She didn't think Mason knew, either, but she hoped he would reach some type of conclusion soon, both about her and about the occult powers that were active in Geiststadt.

There were a few things that Antonia hadn't wanted to discuss with Mason. She didn't think Mason was aware of them, and she didn't want to bring them up if he wasn't.

For one thing, she wondered if Mason had thought what it might mean that she had seen the ghosts of the Hessian soldiers before he did. The Noirs were supposedly the ones with all sorts of powers, but Antonia knew that she possessed them as well—and was, by all appearance, even more powerful than Mason.

She knew that Mason believed he had driven away the spiders in her attic, but she knew that she had done more about that than Mason had. He'd thought she was clinging to him in abject fear, but she had been conjuring the fire as surely as Mason himself.

And finally she wondered about the ghosts of Thomas and Jonathan Noir. Why were they appearing now? Mason had answered the question as far as Thomas was concerned. He wanted MIND-NET, according to Mason, and Antonia was in agreement.

But Jonathan did not want the same thing. It wasn't in his character—as she understood it from the old writings—to want something like that. She believed that Jonathan was trying to warn her of something, but she could not figure out what that might be.

Antonia didn't think it would be wise to discuss these things with Mason because she didn't know where they might lead, and she didn't want them to interfere with her own plans, even though those plans had changed.

She had hoped to charm Mason and perhaps use the secrets of MIND-NET for her own gain, but she no longer felt the same way about anything. The thought of marriage to Mason, which she had told Frederick was out of the question, was now quite appealing to her, and she saw herself helping Mason in his researches, while he did the same for her, both of them working for a common goal.

For some reason, however, Antonia no longer felt any urgency to complete her Special Project, though she did not want to give up her reading in the old volumes in the attic. She felt that there were many more secrets concealed there, and she was determined to find them.

At the same time, she was hopeful that Mason would call and say something about his feelings for her. She knew what they were, but she wanted to hear him express them.

She never for a moment wondered if her new feelings for Mason were entirely her own, or if they had been inculcated in her by someone else, someone who was no longer alive.

Mason was so mixed-up that he didn't know whether he was awake or asleep, alive or dead.

He had been thinking about one of the very things that Antonia had not mentioned to him, and he had arrived at a disturbing conclusion.

He was afraid that the ghost of Jonathan Noir had appeared to Antonia to warn her against Mason.

Mason's understanding of the tales recounted by Antonia was that Jonathan was a protector. He had protected Agatha Noir from Thomas, and now he must be trying to protect Antonia from Mason, who, though he had no clue as to why that might be so, nevertheless believed it.

It was the only explanation that made sense to him. It panicked him to think of it because the more he was with Antonia, the more he knew that he had to marry her. He had never been so strongly attracted to anyone in his life, and he didn't want anything to come between them.

As with Antonia, it never occurred to Mason that there might be some force manipulating his feelings. He had not had enough experience with the occult for that, and he would not have believed it anyway. So while he was still confused about what to do with regard to Thomas Noir's ghost and MIND-NET, he had no doubts about Antonia.

He was going to marry her as soon as possible.

"On, no, you're not," James told him when Mason announced his intentions.

Laura said nothing. She sat quite still and looked at her son with sad fondness.

"I am," Mason said. "I've made up my mind, and there's nothing you can say that will change it. I know that you think the Noirs and Derlichts are natural enemies, but Antonia and I will change all that."

"I don't believe that you can," James said. "The rancor that exists between our families goes back a long, long way. And who knows what kind of offspring you might have? They could be weaklings."

"Or they could be doubly powerful," Laura said.

Mason was glad she had spoken up. He had been expecting her support, for he knew how much she hoped for grandchildren.

"She's right," Mason said, hoping to seize the advantage. "And if I don't marry soon, I'll never marry."

James started to speak, but Mason wouldn't let him.

"I meant what I said. If I don't marry Antonia, I'll never marry. If you want grandchildren, much less thirteen of them, you'd better not have any more objections."

James's face was red, and Mason thought for a second that he might have a stroke, but he breathed deeply several times and then spoke.

"Very well. I can see that your mind is made up. But you have to promise me that you will continue your work with MIND-NET and not let your marriage affect it."

That was an easy promise for Mason to make, and he

did so. Then he said, "There's only one little thing that can cause my plans to fall through."

"And what might that be?" Laura asked.

"I haven't told Antonia about them. She might not want to marry me."

"I can't imagine why not."

"I can," Mason said.

To Mason's surprise, Antonia accepted his proposal without hesitation. It was quite likely the most unromantic proposal in history, but it was good enough for her.

They were in her kitchen, drinking soda. In his nervousness at what he was about to say, Mason had overturned his bottle, and Antonia was wiping up the spill with a paper towel when he blurted it out.

She had not even pretended to think her decision over. She had said, "Of course," and Mason had kissed her. He had been clumsy at that, too, but after a few seconds his awkwardness gave way to passion, and they both believed that they were on their way to perfect happiness.

"I'll have to tell your father," Mason said, after a few more kisses. He was a little breathless. "How do you think he'll react?"

"Why don't we find out?"

Mason agreed that was a good idea, and he sat at the table, twirling his plastic bottle while Antonia went to find her father.

Frederick came into the room, with Antonia right behind him. He was an imposing figure to Mason, with his gray hair and his rigid bearing. For just a second, Mason wondered if he had done the right thing by proposing, but he quashed the doubt as soon as it occurred.

Frederick stood for a moment and looked at Mason without speaking, sizing him up.

Mason stood up, waiting for the verdict.

"Your family and mine have never been friends," Frederick said. "As I am sure you understand."

Mason nodded, not trusting himself to speak.

"Have you discussed this with your own parents?"

"Yes sir, I have," Mason said.

"And what did they have to say about it? I cannot imagine that they favored the idea of your marriage to a Derlicht."

"They were hesitant at first," he said. "But when I told them how I felt, they saw that they didn't have any choice in the matter. It's my decision, not theirs."

"And Antonia's decision."

"Well, yes. I mean, she's already said yes."

"And mine," Frederick went on as if Mason had not spoken.

"Yes, yours, too, of course. I wanted to ask your permission before we made any plans or announcements."

"Rather old-fashioned of you."

Mason hadn't considered it one way or the other. He'd never proposed before, and he didn't know how to go about it any other way.

The corners of Frederick's mouth twitched in the beginnings of a smile.

"I like the old-fashioned ways of doing things," he said. "I think that more young people today should revert to them. Now, is there something that you wanted to ask me?"

"I wanted to ask you for your permission to marry your daughter," Mason said.

Frederick turned to Antonia and took her hand. He marched over to the table with her and placed her hand in Mason's.

"I grant you my permission with great happiness," Frederick said. "I wish only the best for both of you."

Mason felt the tension drain from his body. He looked into Antonia's eyes.

"I know we'll be happy," he said.

CHAPTER TWENTY-FOUR

The next few months were filled with activity for both the Noirs and the Derlichts. Mason had wanted a small wedding, to take place as soon as possible, but it would have been unthinkable for the two youngest children of the two oldest families in Geiststadt to get married without considerable ceremony.

Although Mason's parents weren't entirely in favor of the wedding, they agreed that if there had to be one, it had better be done correctly, so as to give the community what it expected from two such families.

Ceremony calls for planning, and Mason was glad that most of that was up to the Derlichts. He had no desire to worry about appropriate colors, bridesmaid's dresses, invitation lists, showers, flowers, and a thousand other things that he didn't even know about.

Mason's parents planned the rehearsal dinner, and Mason's brothers, none of whom could believe that their little brother, the hermit, was really getting married, planned the bachelor party. All Mason did was try to stay out of the way, something he was good at.

He spent most of his time working on MIND-NET while

trying to keep the ghost of Thomas Noir at bay. On several occasions, Mason had felt the tugging sensation that he'd experienced with the computer monitors, but each time it happened, it had become easier to resist the spirit.

There were other attempts, and they were not all easy to fight off. The most frightening was an assault that came when Mason was asleep and dreaming.

In the dream, he was walking through a dense forest of trees so tall that they cut off most of the sunlight, which fell only in splotchy patches here and there, showing up the forest flooring of rotting sticks and leaves. Mason could hardly see the thick trunks of the trees because of the darkness. The ground beneath his feet was spongy, like potting soil, and it was hard for him to keep his balance.

He was unable to determine his destination, and he did not know if it was near or far, but he sensed that he had to keep walking, for to stop was to invite some terrible doom. He was so tired that he felt he must have walked for days before arriving in the forest. And for all he knew, he had more days to walk before arriving wherever it was that he was going.

The bark of a dog caught his attention, and even as he turned, he knew that it was not a dog he had heard but the barking laugh of Anubis.

Mason spun around, wide-eyed, the fear-sweat breaking out on him because he somehow knew that although he was walking in dream, whatever happened to him there would happen to him in his waking life. And he knew that if he were killed in the dream, he would never awaken.

Thomas Noir was standing beside Anubis at the base of one of the giant trees, a sardonic smile on his face. Though the forest remained dark, Mason saw them clearly in the filtered sunlight, and he thought for a moment that he was looking at his own face instead of that of Thomas.

"You are a hard one to catch, young Mason," Thomas said, smiling, and Anubis barked in agreement. "Your powers are growing. But I have you now, and resisting me this time would prove most futile. You are without help in this realm."

Mason did not see Thomas's lips move, but the voice sounded in Mason's head as clearly as the voice of the Hessian soldier. But this voice Mason could understand. It was the voice of a tempter, but Mason was not beguiled, though he knew what Thomas was after.

"You can't have what I can't give, Thomas," Mason said, trying to make his voice sound strong and confident. He had not expected an attack in his own dreams and the experience was unnerving.

"Oh, but I can, my bonny boy. You are in my world now, will-ye, nill-ye, and you have no way out unless I should choose to release you. And that is not a likely prospect, I might add. Not bloody likely at all. You should not have stopped here, for now you shall never leave this forest of dreams without my permission and assistance."

Mason didn't want to hear any more. He tried to turn

and leave, but he found that his feet were rooted to the ground. Literally. They had grown into the spongy soil, and he had become like one of the trees.

"Release me!" Mason said, trying to break free of the roots his legs had become. "I can't work any faster on MIND-NET and even if I could, it wouldn't help you."

"Your struggle is useless. When first we met, only days ago, you thought that you were dreaming, but you were not. Now you are, but the effect is real. You are mine to do with as I will, and unless you agree to my proposal, what I do to you will not be pleasant."

Mason struggled with the yielding soil, but it held him like a big soft hand.

"What do you propose?" he asked, ceasing his useless exertions.

Thomas laughed, and Anubis gave one of his startling dog-like cries.

"You know well the answer to that question. I want MIND-NET operational," Thomas said when his laughter had ceased. "I want to walk in the world of men again, not as a spirit, but as a man of flesh and blood and feelings."

Mason did not have to ask how long he had to agree to Thomas' demands. He looked down at himself and saw that his clothing was turning to a fibrous green stalk, as thick as the bark on the trees that surrounded him. The stalk was attaching itself to Mason's legs, as vines writhed up out of the ground and wound about him.

"You will not be found in your bed, but elsewhere," Thomas said. "You have never heard of the Corpse

Flower, but the Captain, my father, grew it in his glass house. It was a flower of death, for sure and certain, and it will grow again if you do not help me."

Mason had never heard of a Corpse Flower, though the glass house, or what was left of it, was real enough. Mason felt the tendrils from the soil working their way under his skin and growing into his very veins, sucking the life from him and replacing it with the life of another, more alien kind.

Mason, however, had no intention of giving Thomas what he wanted. MIND-NET was too delicate and too important of a project to give to someone so evil. Helping Thomas access its power would be like setting loose a serial killer. Mason couldn't bring himself to do it, even if it meant he became a Corpse Flower.

He focused his mind and concentrated on trying to reverse the process that was overcoming him, but Thomas's voice cut into his thoughts.

"It would be but a simple feat for me to save you from death. All I ask is that you do the same for me. Release me from the living death that is my afterlife. If you do, all will be well with you. If you do not, then you will be blotted out, in a sense." Thomas turned to Anubis. "Is that not true, oh guide of the dead?"

Anubis turned his snout to the sky and gave a keening bark.

"You will not need Anubis as your guide this time," Thomas said. "You will be found growing on your own property, a strange phenomenon for all to see and wonder at it. None will know from whence it came, but some

who know the old stories, if such remain, will be reminded of the Captain's Corpse Flower. Perhaps a scientist will come to study the plant, to take samples of its
fleshy blossoms. He will be surprised at his findings, I
warrant you."

Mason's arms spread outward and he felt the blooms
that popped out of his fingertips.

"You are becoming quite a lovely flower," Thomas
mocked him. "You will make the people who see you
gasp in awe."

Mason gathered his mental powers and turned them
inward. He let his thoughts race to his legs and to his
toes that had grown into the ground.

"Set me free," Thomas said. "Take me from this place
and return me to the world I long to stride again as a
man strides. Then you shall be freed."

"*Never,*" he hissed from between his clenched teeth. "I
will not help you!"

The ground did not give up its hold, and Mason
wondered if he were destined to become something new
and odd and strange. He hoped that Antonia would for-
give him his failure.

As he thought Antonia's name, there was a change in
the sky above the trees. The clouds ripped apart like rot-
ten cloth, and the sun came through, drenching the forest
in light.

Anubis screamed in pain when the sunlight struck
him, and his skin began to smoke. He cried out again,
and then he fled into the deeper forest, where the sun
could not reach.

"You have more power than I thought, young Mason," Thomas said. "Or it might be that you have the help of another. My meddling brother will pay for this."

Thomas was still in the shade of a great tree, and he did not await the sun's rays. Like Anubis, he turned away and disappeared into the depths of the trees.

And like a nature movie running in reverse, the process which had bound Mason to the earth ran in retrograde motion. The vines receded, his skin softened, his feet came free of the soil.

Mason thought that he saw something above the trees, a face perhaps. Then it was gone, and he awoke in his bed, soaked with sweat, his hands clenched so tightly that his nails had cut into the palms.

He got out of bed and took a shower, and he did not sleep again that night. From that day forward, he slept with a dreamcatcher in his room, and Thomas did not return by the route of dreams again.

Each time Thomas tried something, Mason fought it off. He felt he was stronger and better able to deal with whatever happened, and he began to believe that he was the equal of Thomas Noir or any other supernatural being. However, that feeling did not preclude a good deal of caution on his part.

A few months earlier, he would have scorned anyone who told him that dreams could become real or that ghosts could rise from a flame in an old cemetery. Now he took such things for granted. The scientist in him rebelled at the thought of such a thing having any value, but his senses told him that the things happening to them were all too real. And that the dreamcatcher worked.

Mason tried not to let Thomas's attacks interfere with his work, but he began to fear finishing it before he found a way to keep it from Thomas. He kept trying to improve MIND-NET, and he made some progress, but he knew he was dragging his feet.

Often in the evenings, after working all day in the study or the lab beyond the basement, Mason would meet Antonia, and the two of them would talk about their work. She continued to be interested in MIND-NET, and she was keeping up with her own research.

"How long before you write that paper?" Mason asked one evening.

Antonia was apparently feeling waspish, because she snapped, "I'm working on it. Between you and Dr. Martin badgering me for it, it's a wonder I've been able to concentrate on it at all."

Mason held up his hands in surrender. "Sorry! I was just asking. You haven't let me see any of it."

"I don't like showing my writing until I'm nearly finished. I want to polish it before letting anybody else read it."

Mason couldn't blame her for that. He was reticent about his own work, too, until it was perfected. He hadn't shared everything about MIND-NET even with Antonia in spite of her curiosity about it.

"Well," he said, "when do you think you're going to be nearly finished?"

"*When*," she said, "I'm finished. Have you actually been *talking* to Dr. Martin?"

"Not at all," Mason said. "I'm just interested."

"It's not like I haven't been busy with a few other things, Mason," she said. "I'll finish when I finish, okay?"

Mason nodded, and decided to let the matter drop. Who was he to question his fiancé, when she obviously had a great deal on her mind.

She's probably been busy planning the wedding, Mason thought. God knows she spends enough hours doing research in that attic, too.

CHAPTER TWENTY-FIVE

Antonia had no answer to Mason's question because the truth was that she no longer cared much about the Special Project. The study of urban legends, which had been so engrossing, now seemed stale and unprofitable. She wasn't concerned about the paper she had been writing or even about receiving her degree from NYU. She hadn't written a word of the paper since she had composed the outline for it months before. She'd crossed paths with Dr. Martin by phone and in person several times, but had always dodged his questions or outright lied to him about her plans.

The research she was doing *now*, while related to the earlier work, served a much larger purpose, one that she wasn't ready to share with Mason, even though she loved him and wanted to marry him.

For as Antonia read and learned, she had felt her own power growing. Frederick had been right to set her on the path to reading the family journals, and he had been right that she could well be the one to restore the Derlicht name, though he had not been aware of all the reasons why.

The possibilities of MIND-NET still captivated her, but Antonia no longer cared whether she ever discovered the origin of the many urban legends of Geiststadt, or even the source of all of them in existence. What she had stumbled upon was bigger than that.

Antonia knew her knowledge and newfound powers might complicate her marriage to Mason. She recognized that her psychic strength was much greater than his, and so she chose to keep her research and expanding abilities a secret, hoping that when the right time came, she could tell Mason and he would understand.

Surely he would, she told herself, for she knew that he, too, was changing. He was more confident in his manner, and appeared stronger. Mason's disdain of the supernatural had all but disappeared, and he had told her, with no small amount of pride, of his ability to resist Thomas Noir's attempts at capturing him and forcing him to speed up his work on MIND-NET.

Antonia saw this as a new depth of character in Mason, and she found him even more attractive now than he had been before. But she worried about him. Even though he insisted that he was not afraid of Thomas Noir and his ilk, he avoided going outside almost as obsessively as he had when she'd first met him. He refused to go into his back yard at all, for that was where the Corpse Flower had grown, but he did show her from the library window one day the remains of the glass house.

"My grandfather was a strange man," Mason said. "And an evil one, besides. Thomas must have inherited that evil bent. I wonder about myself sometimes, to tell you the truth. Is the capacity for evil genetic?"

"I don't think you need to wonder about you," Antonia told him. "But I'd be worried about you if you didn't."

Mason sighed. "Heredity can be a terrible thing, that's all," he said.

Antonia looked out at the ruins of the glass house. Winter had given way to spring, and there was a soft rain falling. Drops that hit the library window flattened and slid down it, giving a wavery underwater quality to the scene outside. Antonia could imagine the old sea captain as he sat inside his glass building, gloating over his Corpse Flower. It was almost as if he were there now, and she wondered why his ghost had never appeared in Geiststadt over the years.

She had read about the Corpse Flower only a few days before, after Mason had told her of the dream in which he had been in danger of becoming the Corpse Flower himself, avoiding doing so only because of his strong resistance to Thomas Noir, assisted by what he assumed to be the ghost of Jonathan Noir. Thomas Noir had implied as much in the dream.

What Mason didn't know, and what Thomas didn't, either, was that Jonathan had nothing to do with Mason's escape. The face that had appeared half glimpsed in the ragged clouds had been that of Antonia, who had advanced far beyond Mason and who had entered the dream to save him.

Antonia was not so much afraid of Mason's heritage and what might become of their own heirs as she was of her own growing occult skills.

"Supposing that we dare to take on heredity," Mason

RUSSELL DAVIS

said, unaware of her musings. "How many children do you think we should have?"

Antonia had a feeling that this was leading up to a question she had been expecting.

"We both come from large families," she said, not willing to give a specific answer.

"Does that mean you like large families, or that you don't?"

"Your parents expect you to have thirteen sons," Antonia said, smiling. "That's a little daunting."

"Not just for you," Mason said.

"Are you complaining about the process?"

Mason laughed and assured her that wasn't the case at all. He was more worried about how he'd adjust to being a father to that many kids.

"Your father did it," Antonia said. "And so did mine."

"But both of them had more than one wife."

So that was what was worrying him, Antonia thought. The possibility of one wife not being able to hold up under the strain of having so many children. Well, she couldn't say it hadn't occurred to her as well.

"It's not just your family who wants plenty of children. My father feels the same way."

"I'm not asking about your father."

"I know, and I want to give you an honest answer, but it's not easy when I'm not sure myself. I think we'll just have to get married and let nature take its course. If we're destined to have a lot of children, then we will."

She spoke of destiny casually, and there had been a time when Mason would have either laughed off such a reference or when it would have just slipped through his consciousness without registering. That time was past.

"You really believe destiny has a part in this?"

Antonia smiled at him. "Of course. Don't you?"

Mason nodded. "I hate to admit it, but I do. It's like we were both drawn into this by something else. Just think about it."

Antonia had thought about it before, and yes, she shared Mason's feeling about their meeting and all that had come after. Why, just at the time when she had begun research for the Special Project, had they met? It had been her doing, or so she thought, but Mason had later confessed that his father had been pressing him harder than ever about marriage just before her call.

And there was the matter of the ghostly manifestations by Thomas and Jonathan. Why now? Because she and Mason had gotten together? Because of MIND-NET? Or was there something else going on, something that neither she nor Mason was aware of?

"However it happened, I'm glad," Antonia said.

"So am I," Mason responded. "But I still wonder about it. I don't like the feeling that I'm being manipulated."

He looked out the window at the drifting rain as if he half-expected to see the ghost of Thomas Noir outside, watching them. He turned back to Antonia and continued.

"I mean, I expect my parents to manipulate me. That's what parents do. Or mine do. My father, at any rate. But I don't care for being manipulated by someone I can't even see, much less identify."

"It could be that we're worrying too much. Sometimes two people just fall in love."

"That would have happened no matter what," Mason said. "I don't question that. I couldn't be happier that we met. If we hadn't, I don't know what would have become of me."

"You'd have done fine. You'd have finished your work on MIND-NET and become famous."

"I'm not so sure. I might have given in to Thomas, or I might have become such a recluse that I'd never be able to leave this house."

Antonia didn't remind him that he seldom left it now, other than to visit her. And even at that he preferred that she come to Noir Manor.

"I don't know what I'd have done if I hadn't met you," she told Mason. "Probably I'd become a dried-up old spinster, sitting in the library stacks with a pile of dusty books, trying to find out the origin of another obscure urban legend." She shuddered. "I should thank you for saving me from that."

"I didn't save you. You're too beautiful and vivacious to have wound up like that."

"I appreciate the compliment, but I'm afraid you're wrong. It doesn't matter now. What matters is that we're together." She looked at her watch. "I should get going. My father's expecting me for dinner."

"You could stay here," Mason suggested, sounding hopeful.

Antonia was tempted, but she wanted to get back to Derlicht Haus. Not for dinner. She had other things on her mind. There was more to read in the old books, more to discover about the Noir and Derlicht families, more to find out about her own growing powers. She shook her head. "I'm sorry, Mason. I'll stay another time."

Vying for additional time, he tried changing the subject. "How are the wedding plans coming along?" Mason asked.

Antonia knew what he was doing. He never asked about the wedding plans except to be polite, and then the details bored him senseless. She wouldn't be able to give many, anyway, since she was leaving all that to her father and her sisters. Antonia was too busy with her reading to have much to do with anything beyond choosing the colors and the bridesmaid's dresses.

"Everything's coming together fine," she said.

"Great," Mason said. "Anything I can do?"

"Don't be silly," she said. "My family and I will handle it. Besides, you've got other work to do." Making a point of glancing at her watch, she added, "I've got to go." She gave him a hug and a kiss and left him at the doorway, watching her as she walked away into the rain, her red umbrella over her head.

Antonia was already thinking about what she might discover in the next book she read, or what new powers might unfold within her mind. She could practically feel Mason's desire for her to stay, but other, more powerful things beckoned. Mason, she thought, would have to wait.

Antonia was hurrying home to yet another book she had found in the stacks in her attic. She had been reading all the books relentlessly and taking copious notes, even though she no longer planned to write anything about them. The knowledge they held was not the kind to write about in an academic paper, and academic pursuits no longer held any fascination for her.

A remarkable, though not surprising, discovery she had made was that the more books she read, the more of them there seemed to be. She was certain that there were now books on the shelves that had not been there when she had begun her researches. Her "assistant," whoever that might be, was supplying her with more than she had expected to find.

Even though Antonia had received several calls from Dr. Martin, she no longer felt any desire to complete her graduate work. Certainly she was studying just as hard, applying herself to her research with the same ardor that she had once reserved for the works of Shakespeare or Hawthorne.

But now her studies were of magic. In one of the old books, Antonia had found a piece of parchment more ancient than any book. On it the ink was so faint that she could hardly make out the words, which in any case were not English.

It didn't matter, of course. Even as she looked at the incomprehensible letters, they writhed on the page, then flowed together to form words that Antonia could read. Her ghostly assistant was still providing much needed assistance.

According to the author of the parchment, who was not identified in any way but who Antonia suspected was an ancestor of the Derlicht family, magic was nothing more than powerful psychic ability suitably directed.

All the accouterments of magic—the wands, the charms, the spells, the pendants—were nothing more than fancy trappings with no power of their own. They merely provided focus for one whose psychic ability was weak or undeveloped.

If this was true, Antonia could make herself into one of the most powerful people in the world. Weren't her own abilities increasing daily? Yes, and with the proper focus, she could control not only her future but Mason's as well. She could make their lives whatever they wanted them to be.

All knowledge of any importance was in the books in her attic, there for the taking, and she planned to take it. She couldn't wait to get home and get started.

She hardly noticed the rain that began falling harder than it had all day, or the gathering shadows around her.

CHAPTER TWENTY-SIX

There is a world of reality, solid beneath our feet, where people live and breathe and laugh and die. There is another world, the spirit world, where reality does not intrude, for this world exists out of space and out of time. No life of our sort is found there, no breath of laughter, and no death, for all who dwell there are dead already in the sense that we understand it.

But they are there, nevertheless, in some form or another, and it was one of them who watched as Antonia pored over the dusty leather-bound tomes in the attic of Derlicht Haus.

The watcher knew of other spirits, but there were none of them present at that particular non-existent point at that particular non-existent moment.

The other spirits wrangled among themselves and tried to direct the course of things.

Thomas Noir.

Jonathan Noir.

They thought they could have some influence on the outcome of life in the world of reality.

The watcher knew it was possible that they could, if their power, their *heka,* were great enough.

The watcher believed it was not, as they would discover to their chagrin.

Each of them had his plans, but the watcher's agenda was different from theirs. That might have mattered to them if they had known of it, but they did not. Too caught up in their own schemes, they did not know that there were others of their kind who were working as hard as they. They cared only for their own ambition and had no regard for the fact that others might aspire to different goals.

Let them connive.

Let them scheme.

The watcher would outdo them both.

CHAPTER TWENTY-SEVEN

Antonia, having discovered to her surprise that she was something of a traditionalist when it came to marriage, wanted a June wedding. As for Mason, the month didn't matter, as long as there was a wedding. So they settled on June 4, the first Saturday in the month.

Neither the Derlichts nor the Noirs had been pillars of any church, at least not in the last fifty or sixty years, so a church wedding was not really something that Mason and Antonia wanted. However, there was a non-denominational chapel on the shores of Skumring Kill that had been there since the earliest days of the town.

No one knew the precise date of its construction, but most of those who thought about it at all considered that it had been home to one of the religious denominations that had flourished in Geiststadt's colonial days. And there was no question that it was one of the oldest structures in the town, older even than Noir Manor.

For that reason, the building had been preserved as well as possible, and when deterioration or decay was detected, Geiststadt's historical association stepped in with money to restore it. Both the Noir and Derlicht families had contributed funds toward its repair in the past. It was small but colorful, and it was used for weddings and the occasional funeral.

"We can't possibly fit everybody inside," Mason said when Antonia suggested the old chapel for their wedding.

Antonia explained that she was well aware of that fact. "We'll just barely have room for the families. But we can set up a large tent outside, with folding chairs. We can have a wide-screen TV in the chapel, and they can watch the wedding as well as if they were inside."

"We're going to televise the wedding?"

"Only to the TV set in the tent. It's not as if we're going to put it on a network feed. I've thought a lot about this, and it's what I'd like to do."

Mason, who felt a little guilty since he hadn't thought a lot about the logistics of the wedding, and done none of the planning, agreed. But he worried about the weather.

"It won't be a problem," Antonia assured him. "I've checked the weather statistics for the last one hundred years. The first week in June is almost always perfect. Warm, but not unpleasant. If it rains, the tent will keep everyone dry. We can have the reception on the chapel grounds after the ceremony, and the tent will still be there in case of emergency."

Mason had known the preparations would be elaborate, given that their families were so prominent, but he'd had no idea of the extent of the planning involved. Checking the weather for the past one hundred years? He'd never have thought of it.

But Antonia had, and she'd thought of a lot of other little and large things besides. So the date was set, and the chapel was chosen, and Mason had little to say about it.

Which was just fine with him, because he had other things on his mind, including Thomas Noir, whose visits seemed to have tapered off for some reason. Perhaps it was Mason's growing ability to best him.

"I always fight him off," Mason told Antonia one day, "but I don't think he'll ever give up. Not really. I worry that sooner or later he'll catch me when I'm unprepared and pull me to the bottom of the Mill Pond or some other place, and I won't be able to find my way back."

Antonia was worried, too, but not as worried as Mason. She had been able to help him out so far, though her help had come without his knowledge. She thought that the ghost of Jonathan Noir might have been aiding her. She hadn't bumped into Jonathan again, but she had seen him several times, always at a distance. It was as if he was there to watch over and protect her, and maybe he was.

"After we're married," she told Mason, "it won't be such a problem."

"How can you be sure?"

"Because together we're stronger than any ghost can ever be."

Antonia still hadn't told Mason that her studies had extended into the realm of magic. She didn't think he needed to know that at the moment. Later would be soon enough for a discussion, when he would have a chance to get used to the idea. For the time being she preferred to keep things vague.

"If you say so," Mason agreed, but he looked doubtful.

"Trust me," Antonia said, and they both laughed.

By May it had become obvious that Antonia was not going to complete her Special Project anytime soon. When Mason questioned her about it again, she told him that she had been too busy with her wedding planning to accomplish any academic work, and he felt guilty about not having done more of the preparation.

Antonia promised him that she would get back to work on the project once they were married, but he could tell she didn't really mean it. If he had known where her *real* interests lay, he would have been even more worried about things.

"I'll support whatever you want to do, Antonia," he had told her, "but you're far too talented to spend your days sitting at home playing housewife."

It had been agreed between them that they would live in Noir Manor so that Mason could continue his experiments with MIND-NET there. He already had his lab and computers set up there, and it would have been difficult to move them, especially the lab.

"You don't have to worry about me," Antonia assured him. "I can find plenty of things to do. I'm not going to become some kind of modern Emily Dickinson, hiding out in the upper stories of the house, wearing a white dress, and looking out on the town from a window."

"I hope I don't become like that, too," Mason said.

"You'd look pretty funny in a white dress."

"You know what I mean."

Antonia did know. Mason was getting better about going outside as his confidence both in himself and his psychic abilities grew, but there was always the chance of regression. Especially if he found out how much she'd been "assisting" him against Thomas. Antonia knew that without her, Mason would most surely have been completely dominated by Thomas' will.

"I hope they don't show up at the wedding," he said.

He didn't have to say who *they* were. Antonia knew as well as he did.

"I don't think they'll be there. They wouldn't stand a chance against the two of us, and they know it."

"I'm sure you're right," Mason said. "Everything will be great."

Antonia hoped he was right.

When the day came at last, Mason wasn't worried at all. He was just as happy and excited as any other groom who didn't have to think about the fact that ghosts might show up at his wedding.

At the bachelor party the previous evening, his twelve older brothers had been astounded by his cheerful demeanor.

"Antonia has been good for you," Michael told him. "I thought you were going to fade into the woodwork of the old house by the time you became an old man, but you've come out of your shell a lot since you met her."

Michael was the eldest of the brothers, the one Mason knew the least, but the one who treated Mason most paternally. And why not? He was twenty years older than

Mason, and could easily have been Mason's father for that matter. To top it off, he bore a strong physical resemblance to James.

Mason liked Michael, and he agreed that Antonia had indeed been good for him.

"She's helped me through some rough times," Mason said. "Weird stuff."

"Been seeing the ancestors?"

Somehow Mason managed to not drop the beer he was holding, but it was a close thing.

"How did you know?"

"We've all seen them from time to time," Michael said. "Nobody likes to talk about it, but I know that Mel has, and so has Merv."

"You've seen Thomas?"

"Thomas? No. I don't know much about him. I've seen Jonathan, though. Usually when there's some crisis. You remember when Sally nearly died after our first son was born?"

Sally was Michael's wife, and Mason did remember. She had come back to Geiststadt and stayed in the hospital there for more than a week. Michael had moved back into Noir Manor for the duration, though he spent most of his time at the hospital with Sally.

"Well," Michael said, "that's when Jonathan showed up. He was standing outside her hospital room, as if he were keeping watch. Maybe he was. At any rate, everything turned out all right."

"How did you know it was Jonathan?"

Michael had a sip of his own beer and thought about it.

"You know," he said, "I have no idea. I just seemed to get that impression."

"There was no one with him, not some dog-looking thing, like Anubis from the Egyptian legends?"

Michael gave him a funny look. "Nothing like that. You sure you haven't had too much of that beer?"

"I'm fine," Mason said. "Anubis is just one of those things that turns up with our ancestors."

Michael shook his head. "Not when I see them."

"Thomas is the one I see. He's not like Jonathan."

"If you say so. As I mentioned, I don't know much about Thomas, but Jonathan gets around."

"You've seen him outside of Geiststadt?"

"No, come to think of it, I never have. Only when I'm here, and I usually do come back when there's a crisis of some kind. It's comforting to be home, I suppose."

Mason thought there was more to it than that. He remembered what Antonia had said about certain places having power, and he thought that might explain why the Noirs felt comforted when they were in Geiststadt. They were drawing on that power, whether they knew it or not.

And Mason was sure they didn't. As far as he could tell, his brothers, if they had any *heka* at all, had no idea how to control or use it. He wasn't surprised. Until a few months ago, he had scoffed at the idea, and his brothers were, if anything, more practical-minded than he was.

The bachelor party went on, and Mason drank more beer. He visited with his brothers, and he wondered what Antonia was doing. Then, just before midnight, he saw Thomas Noir.

By that time, nobody else was in much of a condition to notice the strange attire that Thomas wore, but Mason had remained relatively sober. Thomas smiled and beckoned to him.

Mason looked around. People were drinking, eating, laughing, and having a general good time. He didn't sense danger from Thomas, at least not this time, so he made his way across the noisy, crowded room to where Thomas stood near a doorway.

"Greetings," Thomas said when Mason reached him. "I congratulate you on your marriage."

That didn't seem like Thomas. Mason's suspicions were aroused.

"What do you want?" Mason asked.

"Nothing at all. It gives me pleasure to see my kinsmen enjoying themselves."

Mason looked around once again. No one seemed to notice him or Thomas.

"Can they see you?" he asked.

"Only if I allow it, which I do not choose to do at this time. I have a message for you alone."

Mason tried bravado. "Want a beer before you deliver it?"

Thomas didn't smile. He said, "The message is this: Do not think that your marriage to a Derlicht will save you. I shall have what I want from you, MIND-NET operational and in my control, and there is nothing you can do to stop me."

Maybe it was the beer, maybe it was his newfound confidence, but Mason was feeling feisty. He tipped

Thomas a salute with the beer bottle he was holding and said, "We'll see about that, kinsman."

Thomas smiled thinly. "You are a fool, Mason Noir. You believe you know what is going on around you, but you delude yourself. Your powers are not as strong as you believe, and all you see is an illusion. You have no idea of the real reality of your continued existence, nor will you have. You will live—and die—in ignorance."

A chill touched the base of Mason's spine, and he no longer felt so pugnacious. Still, he would have continued his bravado, but he didn't have the chance. When he looked again Thomas was no longer there.

Around the room, the party went on. No one had noticed a thing, not even Mason's brothers. There was laughter and yelling, but Mason didn't join in. He put his beer bottle down on a nearby tray and slipped out of the room.

CHAPTER TWENTY-EIGHT

The next day was everything a bride and groom could have hoped for, sunny and bright, with a cloudless, blue sky overhead. The air was warm, but not too humid, and the trees in full bloom.

The chapel on Skumring Kill was decorated inside and out with flowers, and the tent outside it was a festive yellow. The trees were green with the leaves of approaching summer, and the sound of the rippling kill could be heard even above the conversations of the guests. There was a soft breeze blowing, though hardly enough to disturb the hems of a wedding dress or muss the hair of the bridesmaids.

Just the way Antonia planned it, Mason thought when he arrived there in the car driven by Michael, who was serving as best man. *It just goes to show that a little research and planning will do for you.*

They got out of the car, and Michael hustled Mason to the back of the building, where they entered through a door in the wall. They found themselves in a small anteroom, where the minister was waiting for them. He was a Unitarian whom James Noir knew slightly, and he had been pleased to be asked to perform the ceremony for two such prominent families.

He shook hands with Mason and asked if he had the ring.

"I do," Michael said, taking it from within a fold of his cummerbund and holding it up for the minister to see. The gold band caught the light and glittered.

"Don't lose it," the minister said. "You'd be surprised how often something like that happens."

Michael said he'd be careful, and the minister asked Mason if he had any questions about the ceremony that hadn't been answered. Mason didn't have any.

"Fine, fine," the minister said.

He was an older man, probably around sixty-five, and he had been in Geiststadt for years. Mason had met him once or twice, but he didn't even remember the man's name. He attributed that to nervousness.

"We'll do everything just the way we went over it in the rehearsal yesterday," the minister said. "I can't think of anything that we need to change."

The rehearsal had been the previous morning, and it had gone without a hitch. Mason hoped things would go just as smoothly during the actual wedding. The minister assured him that would be the case.

"I've never lost a groom yet," he said, with an unctuous laugh.

Michael laughed as well, but Mason didn't join in. He listened to the music being played on the little electric organ that had been rented for the occasion. He didn't recognize the tune.

Two more of Mason's brothers, Max and Morton, came

into the room from outside, and the minister went into the chapel.

"How about it, Mason?" Max said. He was two years younger than his brother. "Ready to go?"

"He's ready," Michael said. "He just wants to get it over with."

Mason realized that was true. And he found himself worrying about Thomas Noir. All he needed was for Thomas to show up at the wedding. But there was no sign of him, and it seemed impossible that he would be there on such a beautiful day.

"How are Mom and Dad holding up?" Michael said.

It was a good question, Mason thought. James had given up his opposition to the marriage when it was obvious that Mason was going through with it no matter who approved or disapproved. But he'd made it clear that he wasn't happy about it. Laura wasn't exactly overjoyed, either, but she'd been more or less on Mason's side from the beginning.

"They're doing all right," Morton said. He was the middle brother and sometimes got lost in the shuffle. "Not dancing in the aisles, mind you, but they'll get through it without embarrassing us."

Max peeked out a window. "A white stretch just pulled up in front. Looks like the bride-to-be is arriving."

The words were hardly out of his mouth before a loud peel of thunder shook the entire chapel.

"Holy shit," Morton said. "Did somebody drop the atom bomb on Manhattan?"

"It was just thunder," Max said.

"No way," Morton said. "There wasn't a cloud to be seen out there when we came in."

"It's cloudy now," Max said. He was still at the window. "Have a look for yourself."

The four brothers, looking quite a bit alike despite the difference in their ages, crowded around the small window. Mason saw that the sky, which only minutes before had been and uncluttered blue, was now almost solidly black, covered by heavy low-hanging clouds. A brilliant flash of lightning lit the scene outside like a strobe light for just a moment, and a peal of thunder rattled the glass in the window.

"I knew the weather in New York was changeable," Michael said, "but I've never seen anything like this before."

Neither had Mason, but he thought he knew the cause. Not that he was going to mention it.

"Is Antonia inside yet?" he asked.

"I'll look," Max said. "It's bad luck for you to see her before the wedding."

Mason didn't think it would matter now. Their luck was already bad. Outside the window, the wind began to whip the branches of the trees, and Mason hoped the tent was solidly pegged down.

The rain started then, pelting the chapel so hard that it sounded like bullets striking the roof and walls. It had become so dark that visibility outside was down to nearly nothing.

Max stuck his head in the room. "She's here. They're going to start before the electricity goes off or something."

Wind buffeted the chapel and whined in the old building's cracks and crevices.

"Better get on with it before the place falls in on us," Michael said, and then it was time for them to take their place at the altar.

Max stood beside Michael and looked down the short aisle to the back of the chapel and then out over the crowd. Most of those inside the chapel were family members. When you have two huge families, the aunts, uncles, children, and grandchildren tend to mount up. All the children under fifteen had been relegated to the tent, with appropriate family members appointed to watch them.

The organist began to play the traditional wedding march, another thing Antonia had insisted on, and the bride came forward from the back of the chapel, walking beside her father.

Mason thought Antonia looked as beautiful as he had ever seen her. Dressed in white, with her black hair, she was a powerful vision of loveliness. Even the thunder and roiling clouds outside couldn't dim her beauty, and she positively shone in the lights inside the chapel.

When Antonia reached the altar, the minister asked the traditional question, "Who gives this woman to be married to this man?"

"I do," Frederick said in a strong voice.

Then he held out her hand to Mason, who stepped forward to take it.

The instant that their hands touched, a mighty wind roared through the chapel. The back doors slammed shut with a noise louder than the thunder, and every light and candle in the chapel was extinguished.

For a moment there was total silence. Then people began talking at the top of their voices, and there was a scrambling of feet. Someone was crying. The temperature in the chapel dropped at least twenty degrees.

"What the fuck?" someone yelled.

Mason held Antonia's hand tightly. Neither of them moved.

In the rafters above them a faint light appeared. It hovered there above them, and someone yelled out, "Look up there! What the hell is that?"

Soon everyone in the chapel was staring upward, their faces revealed by the feeble light.

As they watched, the light grew slowly brighter, assuming a vaguely human shape.

There was a sound like raucous laughter, and the shape thinned into a long, narrow fog. Then it plunged downward, heading straight for Antonia.

Thomas! Mason thought. *He's going to kill her*!

Without thinking of what he was doing, Mason threw Antonia to the floor and covered her with his body. He could feel the crinkling of her wedding gown beneath him, but she didn't cry out. She didn't say anything at all.

For just a second or two, Mason thought it was over and that Antonia was saved.

He was wrong. The light wrapped around him in a spiral and then uncoiled, spinning him across the floor like a child's top. He struck the feet of a bridesmaid, one of Antonia's sisters, and knocked her over as if she were a human bowling pin. They tangled together on the floor.

Mason extricated himself, shoved the sister aside, and spun around. The shape was now a brilliant incandescent white tinged with green, and it lit the entire chapel with a dazzling glare. One end of it was as thin as a knife blade, and it seemed to be trying to force itself between Antonia's lips.

Antonia lay on the floor, rigid as a corpse, and Mason thought for one horrifying moment that she was dead.

But then she started to shake. Her arms flopped wildly. Her veil flew off. One shoe went spinning out among the crowd, none of whom seemed to know what to do, not that Mason blamed them. He didn't know what to do either, except to help Antonia.

He crawled across the hardwood floor in her direction but found he could make little progress. It was like crawling through heavy syrup.

As Mason inched closer to Antonia, he began to have difficulty breathing. The atmosphere in the church had turned thick and soupy. The noise of the people in the pews had changed from being crisp and easily distinguished to something slow and lugubrious, like a symphony being played in the depths of the sea.

Mason shut out the sound and concentrated on reaching Antonia. It had become obvious to him that Antonia was somehow fighting the thing that was trying to enter her body, the thing that Mason believed must be Thomas Noir. If he could take control of Antonia, have the power of life and death over her, he could persuade Mason to do anything he asked, including reveal to him the secrets of MIND-NET.

Mason couldn't let that happen. He stopped crawling and exerted all his mental energy, trying to create a shield around Antonia.

As he did so, he noticed that as the darkness and the fury of the storm increased outside, the light inside was growing stronger. The crowd in the chapel screamed in panic and confusion, but Mason ignored them.

Mason looked toward the rafters and saw that another bright shape was forming there. He thought that it must be Jonathan, come again in a time of crisis to prevent Thomas's dark designs. For the first time, Mason was glad to see a ghost.

The feeling didn't last for long, however, as the second spirit bolted down from the ceiling and also tried to enter Antonia, around whose body a storm erupted to rival the one raging outside the chapel.

There was no thunder, no lightning, but there was a roiling spiral of wind that shook the floor of the chapel like an earthquake. A number of the guests fell over in a tangle of curses and screams.

Mason, unable to imagine why even Jonathan was against him, struggled forward toward the miniature tornado, forcing himself to concentrate all his mental powers on keeping the spirits out of Antonia's body.

He knew that Antonia must be fighting the spirits as well, but he didn't know how well-developed her own powers were. He felt that it was up to him to repel the spirits and send them back to whatever realm they came from.

What was their purpose?

Had they come to possess Antonia or to stop his marriage to her?

And were Thomas and Jonathan working together to possess Antonia?

It made no sense to Mason for them to try to prevent the marriage, so he stopped wondering and concentrated his mind to its utmost to fend the sprits off.

At the same time, he began moving forward again. If he could only touch Antonia, he thought, their physical contact might help to increase both their psychic powers.

Before Mason could get to her, the spirit-created whirlwind surrounding her lifted her from the floor and carried her upward toward the rafters.

Mason gathered all his physical strength and lunged through the syrupy air.

He managed to grasp Antonia's wrist. For a moment they were poised there, Antonia hovering nearly three feet off the floor, with Mason holding onto her wrist. He could feel rippling tremors passing through her body as she fought off the encircling spirits, but he also felt a surge of psychic power as he made contact with her. Using the surge, he joined his energy to hers to force the spirits away from her.

It didn't work. If they were weakened, Mason couldn't tell it. They redoubled their efforts to enter Antonia and possess her completely.

Saving her seemed hopeless. The power of the glowing forms was more than anything Mason could bring to bear, even with Antonia's help. She began to rise even higher above the floor, pulling Mason right along with her because he refused to release his grip on her wrist. He didn't care if they pulled her straight up through the roof. He was going with her, wherever they took her.

Below them on the floor lay the wedding bouquet that Antonia had held. Her white veil lay beside it. Mason saw Michael's anxious face as his brother peered up at them, and, momentarily distracted, he wondered if Michael still had the ring.

As if the thought of the ring held some significance, Mason felt himself grow stronger. He was even able to pull Antonia back toward the floor as he sent mental energy at the spirit lights to force them away.

It seemed to Mason that the whirlwind was growing weaker, so he fought even harder. His shoulder burned with the strain of trying to hold onto her, and it felt as if a low voltage current was passing through his entire body. He gritted his teeth against the pain, and tried to tell Antonia to fight harder, but he couldn't tell if she heard him. Her eyes were closed, and her face was drawn taut.

If I have to, Mason thought, *I can save her by myself alone. No damned ghost is going to stop me. Not even two of them are going to stop me.*

The light around the spirits dimmed somewhat, but Mason was tiring rapidly. He didn't know how much longer he could keep up the contact with Antonia as the spirits tried to wrest her from his grip, and he didn't know how much longer he could focus his mind on the task of freeing her from them.

But he kept trying. For how long he didn't know. Time seemed to have slowed to a crawl inside the chapel. The seconds were hours. The minutes were days. Even the sounds of the confused and frightened crowd faded from his mind.

At last Mason knew he could hold on no longer. He tried to call out Antonia's name, but he was unable to do so.

It was as if she heard him. She opened her own mouth to cry out.

No sound passed her lips, however. Instead she exhaled a vaporous mist that became a thin cloud enveloping her and the two warring spirits. For a moment, Mason lost sight of her, and of the spirit-lights that fought to possess her.

Then there was a crack like lightning, and a great line of light shot from one side of the chapel again.

As soon as it faded, the building was once again plunged into total darkness, and Mason felt Antonia slip from his grasp.

Exhausted, he fell to the floor, his thoughts scattered like dust in the wind.

He raised his eyes to the ceiling, but he could see nothing in the darkness. The spirit-lights were gone. Not even the white wedding dress was visible. He wondered if he would ever see Antonia again.

Sound in the chapel began to return to normal. He heard the frightened conversation of the guests, the shuffling of feet, the movement of bodies.

The wind outside ceased to howl, and rain stopped pelting the roof and windows of the chapel.

The temperature was returning to normal.

Mason struggled to sit up. He could still see nothing, but he kept looking toward the ceiling.

Then the lights came on. Even the candles flickered back to life.

Mason blinked twice. Antonia was lying on the floor, no more than a foot from him.

He leaned over and lifted her head. Her eyes opened and stared into his.

"I do," she said.

Mason looked around for the minister, who stood a few feet away, his mouth agape. He wasn't going to be any help. He looked like a man who had just been hit by a brick.

Michael didn't look much better. It was clear that the guests hadn't seen some of the things Mason had, and he wondered what their eyes had told them was happening.

Probably nothing close to the reality of it, he thought. Well, it didn't matter. As far as he was concerned, the ceremony was going to end the way it should.

Looking into Antonia's eyes, he said, "I do."

She gave him a weak smile. They kissed, and then Antonia clung to Mason for a few seconds before she fainted.

CHAPTER TWENTY-NINE

Wealth has many advantages. One of them is that at just a bit more than a moment's notice, a private hospital room can be established in one's home. So Antonia was ensconced in a hospital bed in one of the rooms on the second floor of Noir Manor.

The wedding guests, including all the family members, had been sent home from the chapel with the explanation, concocted by Mason, that the events of the morning had been nothing more than a freak electrical storm.

Mason, still scientist enough to be an expert in the art of rationalization, explained that such odd occurrences were not unknown in Geiststadt, which was true enough.

He went on to tell everyone that there had been an unusual display of St. Elmo's Fire inside the chapel building. While it was true that such phenomena generally occurred around a church spire or a ship's mast, Mason told everyone, they had been known to develop elsewhere, and such had been the case at the chapel. The guests had been treated to an amazing sight, a once-in-a-lifetime event.

He was never sure how many of them bought his explanation, and some of his brothers seemed especially doubtful, but as they had no other explanation, they chose to accept Mason's as being correct.

Antonia, Mason explained, had been under a great deal of stress in the weeks prior to the wedding, stress that was brought on not only by the impending marriage itself but by her work at NYU, where she was completing a master's degree. The excitement of the storm had been more than she could handle, and she was being treated by the Noir family doctor for exhaustion. The doctor had assured Mason that she would be just fine after a day or so of rest.

Everyone more or less accepted that part of the story as well, and although the wedding could not have been judged a success by anyone's standards, the guests went home without having been too disappointed. They all knew they'd never been to a wedding like it, and they were never likely to see a similar one.

One good thing was that most of them had witnessed the tender scene between Mason and Antonia when the lights returned, and so they thought of the two lovers as joined in a marriage of the spirit, if not one that would hold up in a court of law.

Mason made arrangements to take care of that little matter. That evening, after Antonia had regained a bit of her strength the Unitarian minister appeared at Noir Manor in response to a phone call from James Noir. He was shown to the second floor room, where he performed a brief marriage ceremony witnessed by Frederick Derlicht and Mason's parents. Mason and Antonia exchanged rings, Mason having retrieved them at the chapel, and they were presented by a marriage license that was legal in all respects.

When all was wrapped up to Mason's satisfaction, he sent Antonia's father home and told his parents that he would be spending the night in the room with Antonia.

"Not in the bed, I hope," Laura said.

"Why not?" Mason said. "We're married now."

"You shouldn't tease your mother," Antonia told him.

Laura gave her a grateful smile. "He's bad about that. I hope you'll be a good influence on him."

Antonia responded with a wan smile of her own. "I'll try."

While they talked about him, Mason moved a comfortable chair into the room and settled into it.

"Don't tire her," James said. "She needs her rest."

Mason had a feeling James knew more about what had happened than just about anyone else who had been in the chapel, but he couldn't be sure.

"I'll be good," Mason said. "I just want to be here in case she wants anything."

"Be sure to call us if you need help," Laura said, and she and James left the room.

When they were gone, Mason looked at Antonia with affection. He pulled his chair over to the bedside, sat down, and took Antonia's hand.

"This isn't exactly what I had in mind for our wedding night," he said.

"What did you have in mind?"

"I'd better not tell you. I don't want to get you excited. The doctor said that wouldn't be good for you."

"What does he know?" Antonia said, leaning forward so Mason could kiss her. "He's only a doctor."

Mason kissed her cheek and smiled. "We can wait. What I'd really like to have someone tell me is what happened in that chapel."

"So would I. I don't remember much about it, and what I remember, I'd rather forget."

"I think the ghosts of Thomas and Jonathan were there. Thomas was trying to take over your body, and Jonathan was trying to stop him. Or maybe they were fighting over which one of them would get to control you. I can't figure it out."

Antonia sank back against the pillow. "Maybe we should just forget it. We're starting a new life now, and we can leave that old one behind."

Mason wanted to think it was possible to put Thomas and Jonathan in a cabinet and lock them away like some shameful secret. But he didn't really think that was an option.

What *was* an option was a change of subject, so for a while he and Antonia talked about their plans for their delayed honeymoon and how they would spend it, about MIND-NET and how close Mason was to a break-through, about how happy they were to be together.

After a while Antonia drifted off to sleep, and Mason settled back in the chair to pass the night beside her.

Antonia, however, asleep to outward appearances, was not asleep at all. Her mind was awake and alert, ranging through a territory that Mason had never visited. It was a place out of space and out of time, where mortals seldom walked, in fact or in dream.

But Antonia's psychic powers had increased enormously since the events in the chapel. It was as though they had been stored in an iron vault that had been blasted open by her experience. Though she hadn't told Mason, she was no longer quite the same person she had been when the limo had delivered her to the front of the chapel that morning. Mason's psychic powers were like those of a small child when compared to the ones Antonia now had access to.

Antonia could roam free of her body into astral realms, and she had gone there for a purpose. She was seeking the spirit of Agatha Derlicht.

In the vastness of the place where she found herself, it would seem impossible to find anything at all, spirit or material, but Antonia now had the power to send a mental call, not a request but a summoning, a summoning that Antonia believed must be obeyed.

So it was that in a short time (though time did not exist there) Antonia was approached by the figure of a woman with hawk-like eyes. She was lean as a rake. She wore a cap after the fashion of a much older time, and the hair pinned beneath it was white as pure snow, though thick as if Agatha had been a young and beautiful girl. Her forehead was creased, and her face was lined, with a blade of a nose that jutted out like a ship's prow. Her eyes were clear and blue and sharp. Though once she may have had teeth, her mouth was toothless now, drawn in a frown of permanent distaste. She shook with a constant tremor, as if she might have had advanced

Parkinson's though the disease would not have been called that in her lifetime.

"G-greetings, my kinswoman," Agatha Derlicht said.

"Why do you choose to appear in that form?" Antonia asked. "You could be anything you wanted."

"T-this is the way I was in my life at the end of it," Agatha said. "And s-so I choose to be forever after."

The tremor-induced stutter was also unnecessary, but as Agatha had possessed it in life, so it was her choice to retain it in the afterlife.

"W-why did you call me here? W-what is your p-purpose?"

"Why do you ask? You already know the answers."

Agatha laughed, wrapping her arms around her skinny body and hugging herself.

"Aye. I d-do know. I know that, and many things more."

"Then tell me what happened. You were there, weren't you?"

"Oh, yes. Indeed, yes, I was there. As were others. As were others."

"Thomas and Jonathan. Their spirits were fighting for possession of my body."

"Those two." Agatha gave another of her peculiar hugging laughs. "Those two."

"I don't see what's so funny about them."

Agatha stopped laughing and peered at Antonia from beneath her cap, looking her up and down with the hawk-like blue eyes.

"You do not know as much as you think you do, then. Not nearly as much."

"Tell me. Tell me now."

"And do you think you can force me? Me, who remains even now the most powerful of all the Derlichts? Do you think I came at your call because I could not but harken to it? That alone shows how little you know, for I came only at my own bidding, not at yours."

Antonia did not want to argue or engage in a literal battle of wills. She wanted answers, and she decided that it might be easier to get them if she tried politeness.

"I beg your pardon. I didn't mean to be insulting. I was hoping you might be able to tell me something I wanted to know. After all, I suspect you've been guiding me for quite some time now, haven't you?"

Agatha hugged herself and laughed as if Antonia were the very soul of wit. When she had control of herself again, she said, "Aye. I have been with you. I have been with you far more than you know."

Antonia felt atavistic fear at the words.

"What do you mean by that? I know you assisted my studies. Were you with me at other times?"

Agatha laughed. "At all times. All times. And not just you, oh, no, not just you."

Antonia wondered if the old woman might be raving. Was it possible for a ghost to have dementia?

Agatha controlled herself. Her tremors all but disappeared. She said, "Do you think that it was you who controlled your destiny? Did you think that everything that has been happening was caused by some odd quirk of fortune, good or ill? Then think again. Think again."

Antonia could only guess at Agatha's meaning, but her ancestor seemed to want her to say something.

"You mean my marriage to Mason?"

"All of it," Agatha said. "From the very first."

"My Special Project?"

"Aye. That was a beginning. But it was I who put the notion in James Noir's mind that Mason must find a wife. It was I who helped you read the old texts. And I who brought you and Mason together. My doing. All my doing."

Mason had once mentioned to Antonia that he felt somehow manipulated, as if there were a puppet master pulling his strings, but they had laughed off the feeling, glad that they had met no matter what the cause.

And the cause seemed to be Agatha. But was she really behind everything?

"My love for Mason is real," Antonia said. "It has nothing to do with you and your machinations."

"Are you so sure of that?"

Antonia searched her heart. "I've never been more certain of anything. You may have set things in motion, but you have no control over the way people respond to one another."

"So you say. Perhaps you do love Mason Noir, but does he truly love you?"

"He does. I'm as certain of that as of my love for him. There are some things that can't be faked, and one of them is love, at least the kind Mason and I have."

"Very well. Believe what you choose. It has nothing to do with me. Your love does not change a thing."

Agatha looked quite smug, and Antonia wished she could think of some way to shake the old hag.

"If you were in control of everything," she said, "what about those spiders?"

Agatha laughed yet again, as if the thought of the spiders was a merry one.

"My little servants, yes, they do my bidding, both the ones that are real and the ones that are not."

"But why? Why have them attack us?"

"Ah, that was a wonderful time, was it not? I thought it would never come."

"It didn't seem wonderful to me."

"But wonderful it was. It was the real awakening of the power of Mason Noir's mind. He resisted me. He resisted so much that I despaired of having full control. But the precious spiders came to my aid, as did the dead Hessians. All my doing. All."

"You called up the dead men?"

"No. Do not mistake my meaning. The dead men are always there. They have been since the time of the revolution. But I sent you to them. I sent you so that Mason Noir might see and believe."

He did believe, Antonia thought, but there were still a lot of loose ends.

"What about Thomas and Jonathan. Did you send them, too?"

"Only in a way. They are here with me in this place, and they sensed what I was doing. So they went out into the world, but for their own purposes. Not mine."

"What were their purposes?"

"To save Mason Noir. Do you remember how we saved him in his dream?"

"We? I remember, but I thought I saved him."

"Oh, no. It was the two of us who did it. You did not yet have the power, though I believe you have it now."

"We saved him, then. Thomas Noir was after him. With that dog thing."

"That is Anubis, but it is not necessary for you to know about it."

"Fine. Why did you want to save Mason?"

"Because I had other plans. It is my plans that have mattered all along, though I allowed Thomas Noir to think that he might have a chance to further his own schemes. And of course poor Jonathan tagged along to see whom he was going to have to save this time. Once he saved me, you know."

"I know. I read about it. But Jonathan hasn't saved anyone this time."

"No, and he shall not, though he tried. Even Thomas tried, but only when it was far too late for him to do what he thought he must."

"Are you talking about what happened at the wedding?"

"Yes, that is what I am talking about."

"And Thomas and Jonathan were trying to save me?"

"Not at all. Not at all. They were trying to save Mason Noir, their kinsman."

"Save Mason? Save him from what?"

"Why from you, my dear. The were trying to save him from you."

And with that, she was gone.

CHAPTER THIRTY

In the chair beside the bed, Mason tossed as dreams wracked his sleep. Mason could not travel where Antonia had gone, but his dreams took him to places he did not want to be.

In one of the dreams Thomas Noir appeared, calling Mason's name from a great distance. Anubis was not with him, but someone was, and Mason saw that it was Jonathan. He didn't understand what was happening.

In the dream they came closer, covering the distance between them in an instant.

For the first time Mason noticed where they were: HangedMan's Hill. He could look out over the town of Geiststadt, but it wasn't the town of the present. It was the village of the past, and he could see the sun as it reflected off the roof of the Glass House behind Noir Manor.

"What are we doing here?" he asked. "Have you come to make me the Corpse Flower at last?"

"No," said Jonathan. "We are here to tell you that you will see us no more."

"Speak for yourself, brother," Thomas said. "I have not

yet given up my hope of walking again as a man does and going freely to and fro in the world."

"You won't get any help from me," Mason said.

"Nor will I need it. Should I ever come again, I will come with aid that you cannot resist."

"I'm not afraid of Anubis, either."

"You should be," Jonathan said. "Even Thomas fears Anubis, who can guide him to the land of the dead and leave him there, forever extinguished. Thomas does not want that. Even such life as we have is precious to him."

"And precious to you, brother. You relish your watchdog role the way an actor loves the stage."

"What's going on?" Mason said. "That was you at the wedding, wasn't it?"

"It was the two of us," Jonathan said. "For the first time in centuries, we were joined in a common task, and we failed."

"It was your fault," Thomas told him. "Had you let me go alone, I would have succeeded. You have too much regard for the old witch."

Jonathan frowned and shook his head. "I thought that she might have regard for me. But that was not the case. She was strong, far too strong."

"Will one of you please try putting this in terms I can understand?" Mason said.

"I shall try," Jonathan said. "First of all, you will see us no more because we are no longer needed in your world. There was a battle, and we have lost."

"What battle? How did you lose?"

Jonathan ignored the questions. He said, "I was tricked,

and I believe Thomas was tricked as well, though he will be loath to admit it."

"I was not tricked. I still believe."

"This isn't helping me," Mason said. "Start over, at the beginning."

"There is no time for that."

"Then tell me how you were tricked."

"I was not tricked," Thomas repeated. "I will have what I want. I will ..."

"You will not," Jonathan said. "Agatha Derlicht put the thought in you that MIND-NET could allow you a sort of return to life. It is a vain hope."

"It is *not*!"

Jonathan shrugged. "As you will. But I say it is in vain. Agatha was hoping to distract you from her own work, and at the same time distract me, for I believed that your own attempts against Mason were the real danger. They were not. Agatha was, and her distraction worked. When we discovered her true design, it was too late."

"Too late for what?" Mason asked.

"Too late to prevent her from achieving her goal. When we arrived at the chapel, she was so strongly in possession of Antonia Derlicht that there was nothing we could do. And so we will depart."

"I shall not depart," Thomas said.

Jonathan smiled. "I never liked you, Thomas, but I must admire your tenacity in the face of the facts."

Both figured began to go blurry. They were fading like a fog.

"What was Agatha's goal?" Mason asked.

"To have you married to Antonia," came a voice, though Mason could not distinguish whose it was. The figures were indistinguishable now.

Mason shouted one last question before they disappeared completely.

"Why did she want me to marry Antonia?"

The words that came back to him were so indistinct that he could make out only one of them:

"...doom...."

CHAPTER THIRTY-ONE

Mason awoke the next day filled with vague feelings of gloom and despair. He remembered parts of his dream, especially the final word, and became even more depressed.

Contributing to his feelings was the fact that Antonia did not awaken. She seemed to be in some kind of trance, and Mason didn't know if it would be wise to wake her. He asked James's advice, and James called the doctor, who told them that Antonia needed her rest. They were advised to let her sleep.

"I know Mason is eager to have his honeymoon," the doctor said, "but he'll just have to wait."

Mason wasn't worried about his honeymoon. He was worried about Antonia. The dream had disturbed him even more than he wanted to admit.

There had been a time, only a few months earlier, when he would have dismissed the dream as nothing more than a result of the storm in the chapel, but he could no longer do that. He wished he had been in his own room, where the dreamcatcher hung in the window.

He told himself that he would bring it to Antonia's room if he spent another night there.

Around noon, Antonia woke up. She didn't seem refreshed by her long sleep, and she refused to talk to Mason beyond the simplest answers to the simplest questions. He was afraid that she had become seriously ill.

But by later in the afternoon she seemed better. She told him that her sleep hadn't been restful but that she was confident tonight would be different.

"Did you dream?" Mason asked, thinking of his own uneasy sleep.

"No," she answered truthfully. "I didn't dream."

She ate only a little during the day, and shortly after dark she fell once more into an exhausted sleep, or so it appeared to Mason, who had no clue as to her nocturnal adventure of the night before.

But, once again, Antonia did not sleep. She entered another domain, the spirit world, and she was determined to find Agatha again and to force the final truth from her, however ugly it might prove be.

Agatha came again at Antonia's bidding, but this time she was not so jolly as she had been. Her laughter was replaced by a look of melancholy sadness.

"You should not have returned here," she told Antonia. "And having returned, you should not have summoned me. You do not want to hear anything further I have to tell you."

"That's where you're wrong," Antonia said. "You're

going to tell me what you meant about Jonathan and Thomas trying to save Mason from me, or else."

"Or else? You are in no position to say such things. You should learn the limits of your power, and you should learn that there are some cases in which ignorance is preferable to knowledge."

Antonia's scholarly nature rebelled at such an idea. She said. "I always prefer knowledge to ignorance. So tell me."

Agatha looked at her with compassion, as if she regretted having to give the answer Antonia craved.

"Had you been born in my time," she said, "I could have liked you, for you are tenacious and not easy to intimidate. Let me say first that you were only a tool in this great game of mine. It is too bad you had to be the one."

The words were no comfort to Antonia, and she feared what Agatha had to tell her, but she did not relent.

"I want to know, no matter what."

"Very well. Here is the truth. Jonathan and Thomas wanted to prevent the marriage because they did not want the thirteenth Derlicht daughter to be joined to the thirteenth Noir son. It is as simple as that."

Antonia didn't get it. "But why? Mason says that his father has been encouraging him to marry for a long time. And my own father was eager for me to marry Mason."

"As I told you, I was the motivator. In everything."

"But you never told me why."

"And for good reason. But I will tell you now. Both families, as you know, wanted their thirteenth child to marry. Both believed that good would come of it. James Noir was wary, however, of having his son marry a Derlicht, and well he might have been. Your father, on the other hand, thought your marriage to Mason Noir would be a good thing. And there was a reason for that, as well, though it was not the reason that your father believed it to be."

Antonia shook her head. "This still isn't making sense."

"Be patient. You have read the books in the attic. You have seen that their words have invariably been true. Is that correct?"

Antonia admitted that it was.

"Very well, then. Believe that what I tell you now is true. The prophecy that overrules all is this one: your marriage to Mason Noir has sealed the doom of his family forever."

Antonia's heart sank. "Doom? How can that be?"

"I will tell you only because there is nothing you can to do change it. If a single child is born to the thirteenth daughter of the Derlicht line and the thirteenth son of the Noir family, it will be the last of the Noirs. There will be no more. That will be the end."

"What? How?" Antonia asked.

"Watch," Agatha said. "Watch and see."

A cloud passed over Antonia's vision and she saw him...it. The thing that would come should she and Mason have children. It looked perfect, almost too perfect. A child of hair the color of a wet raven's wing and eyes so green they looked like emeralds. But the child's aura...

In her mind, Antonia cried out. The child was pure evil and would bring about the ruin of everything the

Noir's had built—including MIND-NET, which would be used strictly for it's own ends.

It wasn't a child, Antonia realized. It was a monster imbued with the cruel, selfish spirit of Thomas Noir himself.

"You're lying," Antonia said.

"As you wish. But I have told you nothing here but the truth. Jonathan and Thomas discovered it, but too late to stop the marriage. They hoped to possess you and thus command you to leave the chapel before completing your vows. They almost succeeded. You and Mason were not quite strong enough to fight them off, but with my help you succeeded. Now you are married. The end is clear."

Antonia thought hard, and came to a way out.

"Not if we don't have child," she said.

Now, Agatha changed to the laughing crone she had been previously.

"Not have a child? But your husband wants a child. He wants thirteen of them."

Antonia knew the truth of it, and she felt hollow inside. She saw her future stretch out before her, dark as night and barren as a desert.

"There is a way," she said.

"No," Agatha said. "There's not. The Noirs have lost for all time."

In her mind, Antonia visualized her womb, and thought of the children she would never bear. The hurt it would cause Mason. She felt unbearable sadness, but there was no other choice. She had to do it. Focusing her energy, she traced the hidden pathways of the body. The magic of conception, what makes a sperm and an egg create the miracle of life, would never be hers. Thrusting with a mental knife of fire, Antonia burned away the eggs stored within her body, searing the fallopian tubes with an energy that no physician would ever be able to see—or heal.

A burning sensation heated her stomach, and in her anger and hurt, she hurled the image at Agatha.

"No!" Agatha cried, "You mustn't! The Noirs must be beaten. I've waited so long!"

"Begone," Antonia said, gasping in pain, "and never show yourself in Geiststadt again."

"You still think you have the power to command me?"

"What I have done cannot be undone," she said. Antonia raised her hand, palm outward. "Now begone...or be banished."

"As you wish," Agatha said, and disappeared.

Antonia sat up in the bed. She looked around the darkened room and saw Mason, asleep in the chair beside her bed.

She had spoken to him of destiny, but she hadn't known what destiny had in store. It was crueler than she could have guessed. Would the Noir line end with them? Perhaps not if MIND-NET came to fruition. In time, perhaps she and Mason could have children of a sort, or perhaps they could adopt.

Mason stirred in his sleep, and she thought about waking him to tell him what she had learned, that she could never give him the family he wanted, that his parents wanted, that everyone expected.

Would it be fair to tell him? she wondered. He would find out soon enough without any words of her own.

It was impossible to say if it would be better to crush his hopes at the outset of their marriage or wait until later.

Sooner or later, however, they would have to confront the truth. Their ancestors, hers in particular, had played with them like chess pieces, but the outcome wasn't what they'd hoped for. Agatha, finding at last the means of her long desired revenge against the Noirs, had been thwarted, but at a terrible cost. And the ones Agatha had truly hated were long dead. They would not suffer. Antonia and Mason would do that in their stead.

It wasn't fair, Antonia thought, and a tear ran from the corner of her eye down her cheek.

Just at that moment Mason woke up. He sat straight in the chair and looked at Antonia.

"You're crying," he said. "What's the matter?"

Antonia looked at her husband, the tears flowing freely down her face, and found the strength to lie. "It's just that I'm so happy," Antonia said. "It's just that I'm so very happy."

EPILOGUE

There is a place that is not a place.

It exists on the fringes of our own reality, and time is meaningless to those who reside there. Powerful creatures whose plans often transcend the ability of man's mind to grasp lurk in its shadows, dance in air spirals on its hot sands.

One who lived there, once called Thomas, watched his descendents. His feelings of rage grew as time, such as time is in a place that is not a place, passed.

But he could wait. His plans were evolving.

His turn, his time, would come again.

In a place that is not a place, one who was once called Jonathan, brother to Thomas, also watched. He watched his descendents, but mostly he watched Thomas.

Thomas was evil and would not give up his desire to return to the realm of man—not as a spirit, though, but as a creature of flesh and blood. Jonathan knew he could not discern Thomas's plan in advance; he would have to wait and react when the time was right.

And Jonathan also knew he would be there to try and

stop him. He understood Thomas, his desperate want to *feel* again.

But for now, whatever now means in a place that is not a place, he could watch and wait. Because in the town called Geiststadt, where strange things occurred or were seen, the battle between them would come again....

COMING JANUARY 2004

THE TWILIGHT ZONE
BOOK 3: DEEP IN THE DARK
by John Helfers
ISBN: 0-7434-7978-5

THE EXCITING CONCLUSION TO THE FIRST-EVER TWILIGHT ZONE TRILOGY!

It is the year 2159, and much like today, mankind has seen radical advancements and horrifying setbacks in the past 150+ years. Earth has become even more urbanized, but with 28.5 billion people on the planet, there are new problems to find solutions for. Crime and overpopulation are major concerns, but the biggest problem facing the planet is the overtaxed environment, which is ozone-depleted and deforested, even in North America. Ultraviolet alerts are common, and the average temperature rose several degrees before being brought under control, also causing occasional flooding problems in the lower areas of New York City, which has been built up to protect it from the ocean.

On New Year's Day, 2159, Mason Noir (III), looking exactly as he did in the year 2002, receives a message from his technicians: they are ready to begin "the procedure." Decades of research have finally come to fruition, and just in time, as this year is the beginning of a new age for mankind...